WESTERN WP PROMISES

✓ SHIPMENT 1

Cowboy Sanctuary by Elle James
Dade by Delores Fossen
Finding a Family by Judy Christenberry
The Family Plan by Cathy McDavid
Daddy's Double Duty by Stella Bagwell
The Sheriff's Son by Barbara White Daille

✓ SHIPMENT 2

A Bride for a Blue-Ribbon Cowboy by Judy Duarte
A Family for the Rugged Rancher by Donna Alward
The Doctor Wore Boots by Debra Webb
A Cowboy's Redemption by Jeannie Watt
Marrying Molly by Christine Rimmer
Frisco Joe's Fiancée by Tina Leonard

✓ SHIPMENT 3

Dancing in the Moonlight by RaeAnne Thayne
One Tough Cowboy by Sara Orwig
The Rancher's Runaway Princess by Donna Alward
A Taste of Paradise by Patricia Thayer
Her Cowboy Daddy by Cathy Gillen Thacker
Cattleman's Honor by Pamela Toth
The Texan's Secret by Linda Warren

SHIPMENT 4

Fannin's Flame by Tina Leonard
Texas Cinderella by Victoria Pade
Maddie Inherits a Cowboy by Jeannie Watt
The Wrangler by Pamela Britton
The Reluctant Wrangler by Roxann Delaney
Rachel's Cowboy by Judy Christenberry

SHIPMENT 5

Rodeo Daddy by Marin Thomas
His Medicine Woman by Stella Bagwell
A Real Live Cowboy by Judy Duarte
Wyatt's Ready-Made Family by Patricia Thayer
The Cowboy Code by Christine Wenger
A Rancher's Pride by Barbara White Daille

SHIPMENT 6

Cowboy Be Mine by Tina Leonard
Big Sky Bride, Be Mine! by Victoria Pade
Hard Case Cowboy by Nina Bruhns
Texas Heir by Linda Warren
Bachelor Cowboy by Roxann Delaney
The Forgotten Cowboy by Kara Lennox
The Prodigal Texan by Lynnette Kent

SHIPMENT 7

The Bull Rider's Secret by Marin Thomas
Lone Star Daddy by Stella Bagwell
The Cowboy and the Princess by Myrna Mackenzie
Dylan's Last Dare by Patricia Thayer
Made for a Texas Marriage by Crystal Green
Cinderella and the Cowboy by Judy Christenberry

SHIPMENT 8

Samantha's Cowboy by Marin Thomas
Cowboy at the Crossroads by Linda Warren
Rancher and Protector by Judy Christenberry
Texas Trouble by Kathleen O'Brien
Vegas Two-Step by Liz Talley
A Cowgirl's Secret by Laura Marie Altom

WESTERN WP PROMISES

Texas Cinderella

USA TODAY Bestselling Author
VICTORIA PADE

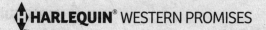

HARLEQUIN® WESTERN PROMISES

Special thanks and acknowledgment to Victoria Pade for her
contribution to The Foleys and the McCords miniseries.

Recycling programs
for this product may
not exist in your area.

ISBN-13: 978-0-373-00343-3

Texas Cinderella

Copyright © 2009 by Harlequin Books S.A.

www.Harlequin.com

Printed in U.S.A.

Victoria Pade is a *USA TODAY* bestselling author of numerous romance novels. She has two beautiful and talented daughters—Cori and Erin—and is a native of Colorado, where she lives and writes. A devoted chocolate lover, she's in search of the perfect chocolate-chip-cookie recipe.

For information about her latest and upcoming releases, visit Victoria Pade on Facebook—she would love to hear from you.

Books by Victoria Pade

Harlequin Special Edition

The Camdens of Colorado
To Catch a Camden
A Camden Family Wedding
It's a Boy!
A Baby in the Bargain
Corner-Office Courtship
Her Baby and Her Beau

Montana Mavericks: Rust Creek Cowboys
The Maverick's Christmas Baby

Northbridge Nuptials
A Baby for the Bachelor
The Bachelor's Northbridge Bride
Marrying the Northbridge Nanny
The Bachelor, the Baby and the Beauty
The Bachelor's Christmas Bride
Big Sky Bride, Be Mine!
Mommy in the Making
The Camden Cowboy

Montana Mavericks: Striking It Rich
A Family for the Holidays

Visit the Author Profile page at Harlequin.com for more titles

Chapter One

"Sometimes I don't understand you, Blake. You open up enough to let me know the business is in a slump, that you think we really can find the Santa Magdalena diamond and use it to pull us out of the fire. But you bite off my head for asking how things are going."

Tanya Kimbrough froze.

It was nearly eleven o'clock on Friday night and she had no business doing what she was doing in the library of the Dallas mansion of the family her mother worked for. But her mother had gone to bed and Tanya had known the McCords were all at a charity symphony that should have kept them out much later than this. And she'd gotten nosy.

But now here she was, overhearing the raised voice of Tate McCord as he and his older brother came into the formal living room that was just beyond the library. The library where she'd turned on the overhead lights because she'd thought she would be in and out long before any of the McCords got home…

Make a run for it the way you came in, she advised herself.

She certainly couldn't turn off the library lights without drawing attention since the doors to the living room were ajar. But maybe Tate and Blake McCord would only think someone had forgotten to turn them off before they'd left the house tonight. And if she went out the way she'd come in, no one would guess that she'd used her mother's keys to let herself in through the French doors that opened to the rear grounds of the sprawling estate. If she just left right now…

But then Blake McCord answered his brother and she stayed where she was. What she was listening to suited her purposes so much better than what she'd already found on the library desk.

"Finding the Santa Magdalena and buying up canary diamonds for a related jewelry line are in the works," Blake was saying. "And we've launched the initial Once In A Lifetime promotional campaign in the stores to pamper customers and bring in more business. That's all you have to know since you—and everyone else—are on a need-to-know-only basis. Your time and interest might be better spent paying some attention to your fiancée, wouldn't you say?"

"What I'd say is that *that* isn't any of your business," Tate answered in a tone that surprised Tanya.

The sharp edge coming from Tate didn't sound anything like him. The brothers generally got along well, and Tate had always been the easygoing brother. Tanya's mother had said that Tate had changed since spending a year working in the Middle East and suddenly Tanya didn't doubt it.

"It may not be my business, but I'm telling you anyway because someone has to," Blake persisted. "You take Katie for granted, you neglect her, you don't pay her nearly enough attention. You may think you have her all sewed up with that engagement ring on her finger, but if you don't start giving her some indication that you know she's alive, she could end up throwing it in your face. And nobody would blame her if she did."

Katie was Katerina Whitcomb-Salgar, the daughter of the McCord family's longtime friends and the woman everyone had always assumed would end up as Mrs. Tate McCord long before their formal engagement was announced.

"You're going to lose Katie," Blake shouted, some heat in his voice now. "And if you do, it'll serve you right."

"Or it might be for the best," Tate countered, enough under his breath that Tanya barely made out what he'd said. Then more loudly again, he added, "Just keep your eye on finding that diamond and getting McCord's Jewelers and the family coffers healthy again. Since you want to carry all the weight for that yourself, you shouldn't have a lot of spare time to worry about my love life, too. But if I want your advice, I'll be sure to ask for it."

"You need someone's advice or you're going to blow the best thing that ever happened to you."

"Thanks for the heads-up," Tate said facetiously.

And then there were footsteps.

But only some of them moved away from the library.

The others were coming closer...

Too late to run.

Tanya ducked for cover, hoping that since she was behind the desk whoever was headed her way wouldn't be able to see her when he reached in and turned off the lights.

"Tate hasn't even been staying in the house since he got back. He's living in the guest cottage..."

Tanya's mother's words flashed through her mind just then and it struck her that merely having the lights turned off might not be what was about to happen. That Tate might use the library route to go to the guesthouse that was also out back....

Tanya's heart had begun to race the minute she'd heard the McCords' voices. Now it was pounding. Because while she might have been able to explain her presence in the library at this time of night, how would she ever explain crouching behind the desk?

Or holding the papers she'd been looking through—because until that minute she hadn't even realized she'd taken them with her when she'd ducked.

Please don't come in here....

"What the hell?"

Oh, no...

Tanya had tried to turn herself into a small ball but when Tate McCord's voice boomed from nearby, she raised her head to find him leaning over the front of the desk, clearly able to see her.

This was much, much worse than when she was six and had been caught with her fingers in the icing of his twin sisters' birthday cake. His mother, Eleanor, had been kind and understanding. But there was nothing kind or understanding in Tate McCord's face at that moment.

Summoning what little dignity she could— and with the papers still in hand—Tanya stood.

It was the first time she and Tate McCord had set eyes on each other in the seven years since Tanya had left for college. And even before that—when Tate had come home from his own university and medical school training for vacations or visits while Tanya still lived on the property with her mother— there weren't many occasions when the

McCord heir had crossed paths with the housekeeper's daughter. Plus, Tanya had been very well aware of the fact that, more often than not, when any of the McCords had seen her, they'd looked through her rather than at her.

So she wasn't sure Tate McCord recognized her and, as if it would make this better, she said, "You probably don't remember me—"

"You're JoBeth's daughter—Tanya," he said bluntly. "What the hell are you doing in here at this hour and—"

He glanced down at the papers and held out his hand in a silent demand for her to give them to him.

She did and he looked over what—before she'd been interrupted—she'd discovered to be some sort of mock-ups for ads for a suggested line of jewelry using canary diamonds set in old Spanish designs.

Tanya had taken the papers from a file that was still open on the desk in front of her. After Tate McCord's initial look at them, he pulled the entire file toward him to see what else she might have gotten into.

While he sifted through what she already knew were similar pages, Tanya was wishing she wasn't dressed in a shabby, oversize, cut-up old sweatshirt and a pair of drawstring black pajama pants with cartoon robots printed on them. She also wished she wasn't completely makeupless and that her shoulder-length espresso-colored hair wasn't pulled up into a lopsided ponytail at the top of her head. Looking as if she were ready for bed made her feel all the more at a disadvantage. When she realized that the wide neck of the sweatshirt had fallen from her shoulder, she tugged it back into place.

It was something Tate McCord saw because just as she did it, he raised his gaze from the file and eyes that were bluer than she remembered drifted momentarily in that direction.

Noticing did not, however, change his attitude toward her—his expression remained stern and angry.

"So, I repeat—JoBeth's-daughter-Tanya, what the hell are you doing in here, at this hour, going through things that you have no right to go through?" Tate McCord finished by tossing the papers he'd taken from Tanya back in the open file.

"I know this can't look good," she said.

But he definitely did look good! Better even than she remembered him.

Unlike her in-for-the-night apparel, he was dressed in a dark suit that accentuated the fact that he was tall and lean, with broad shoulders and a more toned, muscular physique than he'd had in his earlier years. His face had matured into sharply defined angles that gave him a decisive chin and high cheekbones. His mouth at that moment was a stern line beneath a strong, thin nose and his penetrating, clear blue eyes seemed to have taken a bead on her, which should have kept her from thinking that she liked his dark blond hair slightly longish, the way he was wearing it now....

But it was the expression that said he was waiting for an explanation that she knew she really had to address.

"My mother dropped her sweater when she came through here today after she finished work—" Tanya pointed to the plain white cardigan that had been her excuse for this foray. She'd picked it up from the floor where it had fallen and tossed it across the back of a chair before beginning her snooping. "Mom likes to wear it when she walks over from the bungalow in the mornings.

She was just going to leave it and get it tomorrow, but I thought I'd come back for it tonight so she'd have it."

All true, but feeble at this point. Very feeble.

"And while you were here, you thought you'd take a look around, at things that you shouldn't look at, and then hide under the desk so you didn't get caught eavesdropping on what Blake and I were saying in the other room? Or are you going to pretend you didn't hear anything?"

There was that facetious tone again. It could be harsh. And it didn't help that his assumptions of what she'd done were right.

Maybe offense was the best form of defense....

"I heard enough to know that there's a whole lot going on. That all the suspicions about McCord's Jewelers' business being way down have some foundation. That the rumors that the McCords came into possession of the Santa Magdalena diamond when you all got the Foley's land and silver mines could also be the truth. I heard enough to know that your family does think the diamond can be found."

"So you heard plenty."

"And I'll admit," she continued, "that

when I came for Mom's sweater and saw the file, I got curious, and since it was open I looked at those pages—" That was a lie, not only had she opened the file herself, but she'd come to get the sweater hoping that there might be something of interest to her in the library where business was sometimes conducted. "But now that I know things are popping here, it seems to me that there's a story in it that I could use."

"You're going to make me sorry I did what your mother asked and send your résumé over to my friend at WDGN, aren't you?"

WDGN was one of the local independent news stations.

"I didn't know which of you got me the interview, but thanks for it," she said as if that mattered at this point.

"Oh, believe me, you're welcome," he said snidely.

"But here's the thing—" she went on, ignoring his disapproval "—I've been making my living in the world of broadcast journalism for a while now and this is how it works—at least for me because I haven't made any kind of big splash yet—a new position means I start at the bottom. The bottom is filling in for other reporters or doing whatever the seasoned reporters have moved on from or refuse to do—"

"Was I supposed to see if I could have you hired at the top?"

"That's not what I'm getting at. What I'm getting at is that between the story of the diamond—whatever it might be and especially if you do actually find it—and the story of the McCords' feud with the Foleys, well, let's face it, if the McCords or the Foleys sneeze it makes the news so stuff like this could get me an anchor chair." Not to mention the other tidbit the staff was whispering about that *wasn't* public knowledge—that Tate's mother, Eleanor, had an affair with Rex Foley and that the youngest brother, Charlie, was Rex Foley's son....

If Tate's sky-blue eyes had had a bead on her before, it was nothing compared to the way they were boring into her now and it made Tanya's tension level rise another notch. Especially when she began to wonder if she'd gone too far. The McCords *were* her mother's employers after all....

Then Tate McCord said, "Or how about a story where the housekeeper's daughter gets arrested for breaking and entering, for trespassing, for who knows what else should something turn up missing...."

Tanya took issue with that last part. She might be willing to do a little nosing around for a story, but she wasn't a thief!

"Should something turn up missing?" she repeated. "Go ahead, look around. Take inventory. I haven't so much as touched anything but my mother's sweater and the papers in that file. I have done almost nothing wrong!"

"Almost nothing wrong?" Tate took a turn at parroting in the midst of a wry laugh. "Believe me, with the McCord connections, *almost* can still get you arrested. And how would your mother like to hear that you're using the trust we have in her to do something like this?"

"You're threatening to tell my mommy?" Tanya said with some sarcasm of her own even though the threat to tell JoBeth carried more weight than the threat to call the police.

Tate didn't respond to her flippancy. He merely glanced down at the file again, closing it and laying his hand flat on top of it as if that could seal it away from her.

Then those eyes pinned her in place again

and he said, "I'll tell you what this family *doesn't* need right now—a traitor in our midst."

"I'm hardly that," Tanya countered, chafing under that comment more than anything he'd said yet.

"So it's loyalty that brought you in here tonight?"

There was that facetiousness again.

"I was just hoping for an inside story. The discovery of that sunken ship that the Santa Magdalena supposedly came from has renewed interest in the diamond and I thought—"

"That you'd use your mother's position here as a way to get the scoop."

Despite pretending not to take seriously his threat to bring her mother into this before, Tanya was becoming increasingly worried that she'd done damage to the position that her mother had held since Tanya was barely two years old. She definitely didn't want that.

"I'm sorry, okay?" she conceded. "I shouldn't have—"

"No, you shouldn't have. But now that you have—"

"Fine. If you want to have me arrested then do it. But leave my mother out of it.

She doesn't have anything to do with this. She's sound asleep and doesn't even know I'm here or that I had any intention of coming over here."

He seemed to consider that and Tanya had started to wonder how the robot pants and *Flashdance* sweatshirt were going to go over in jail when he said, "I'll make a deal with you."

Tanya raised her eyebrows at him and waited.

"I'll keep your secret about this little escapade tonight if what you heard and saw here, stays here."

Jail in robot pants and a *Flashdance* sweatshirt was easier to accept.

"You want me to just sit on the fact that the McCords honestly *do* believe they have the Santa Magdalena diamond?" she said incredulously. "That you're so convinced of it that your brother is planning the family's business future around it?"

"That's exactly what I want you to do."

"I think *that's* unfair of you!" Tanya said with a little heat in her own tone now. "This is something that could make my career and you want me to do nothing with it when we both know it's going to come out sooner or later, and potentially be a coup for someone else? I'll grant you that I may have stepped over the line using my mother's position here, but I don't think I should be penalized because she works for you."

Tate McCord gave her the hard stare. But if he thought she was going to back down because of it, he was mistaken.

Maybe he saw that in the fact that she didn't waver in the stare down they were engaged in because he took his hand from the file, stood straight and said, "Okay, how about this—whether or not we do have the diamond and where it might be and if it can be found are all questions that have yet to be answered with any kind of certainty. What you think Blake is planning the business's future around is really—honestly—a gamble we're taking. But if—big *if*—we should end up finding the diamond and everything pans out, I'll promise you an exclusive."

"In other words, you want to buy some time," she said.

His eyebrows were well shaped and one of them rose in reply.

"My price is higher than that," Tanya said, deciding that if she was in for a penny, she might as well be in for a pound.

"Your *price?*" He was obviously astounded by her audacity.

But Tanya didn't let that daunt her. "I want the whole story—and I mean the *whole* story, so that if the diamond ends up being a bust, I'll still have something to launch me. Like I said before, if the Foleys or the McCords sneeze, it's news. But there are a lot of details and history and background that even I don't know. And if I don't have the complete picture after growing up here, I have to think not many other people do either. So it can give meat to the bigger story of the Santa Magdalena diamond finally, actually, being found. Or it can at least give me a well-rounded, juicy human-interest piece about Dallas's two most illustrious— and infamous—families. And why they hate each other."

"What kind of details, history and background are we talking about?" Tate said in a negotiator's voice.

"Inside information on the family—the personal things that haven't been in press releases. I want to know about the feud with the Foleys—the truth. I want to know all about the McCord jewelry empire—including if it's hurting. I want the full package, enough to make it interesting even if it turns out that the search for the diamond is nothing but a wild-goose chase."

"Meat," Tate repeated the word she'd used moments before. "You want to treat us like meat."

"I just want the truth and not what's already common knowledge. Think of it this way, you got me a job at an independent news station that *isn't* owned by the Foleys so there won't be any pressure to make you guys look bad. My mom works for you, I grew up here—if anyone will do the story without painting you in a bad light, it's me."

"Or I could just have you arrested and fired and—"

"And then I could go to one of the Foley-owned stations or newspapers or what have you and do the story from their angle."

Once more Tate McCord stared at her long and hard.

"You know, I *like* your mother."

Meaning he *didn't* like her. Tanya had absolutely no idea why that bothered her. But it did.

Still, she wasn't about to show him so she merely raised her chin in challenge.

Then he surprised her and laughed. "And I'm assuming I get to be your source?"

"You're the one proposing we make a deal."

She wasn't sure if he liked that answer or if he had something up his sleeve, but he smiled and said, "All right. Deal—you keep quiet for now, I'll give you the inside story and the exclusive on the diamond if we find it."

He held out his hand for her to shake.

Tanya took it, clasping it firmly to let him know she wasn't intimidated by him.

But what she hadn't anticipated was how aware she would be of the way her hand felt in his. Of the strength emanating from his grip. Of the texture of his skin. Of the tiny goose bumps that skittered up her arm...

Then the handshake ended and something made her sorry it had.

But that couldn't be...

"For now I guess I'll just say good-night, then," Tanya said, thinking that in all that had happened since she'd first heard Tate McCord's voice this evening, she hadn't wanted to get out of there as much as she did at that moment, before anything else totally weird came over her. Or overcame her...

"Good idea," he confirmed.

So Tanya stepped from behind the desk, snatched her mother's sweater from the back of the chair on her way to the French doors and finally went back out into the night air.

And the entire time she held her head high, knowing that Tate McCord had followed her to the door to watch her go— probably to make sure she did, she thought.

But it also occurred to her, as she took the path that led through the woodsy grounds to the housekeeper's bungalow she was temporarily sharing with her mother, that she wasn't sure what her mother and the rest of the staff were talking about when it came to Tate. He didn't seem dark and brooding and withdrawn and dispirited to her.

To her, he seemed full of life, full of fire.

Fire enough to have nearly set her aflame with a simple handshake…

Chapter Two

A good night's sleep had been hard for Tate to come by in the last year and a half, and Friday night hadn't broken that pattern. He'd had trouble falling asleep and he was wide awake before the sun was even up on Saturday morning. And once he was awake there was no going back to sleep. Luckily he'd gotten used to functioning on only a few hours' rest during internship, residency and surgery fellowship.

By 6:45 he'd made himself a pot of coffee and he took his first cup out of the guesthouse to sit at one of the poolside tables with the newspaper that Edward—the McCord's butler—hadn't failed to leave at his doorstep since he'd returned from the Middle East and opted to live outside of the main house for a while.

Tate didn't open the paper, though. He knew there would be articles on the war in Iraq, on situations in Pakistan, Afghanistan and Lebanon. Unlike when Buzz had been over there and Tate had been anxious for any news, since Buzz's death, since spending the year in Baghdad himself, some days he just didn't want the reminders. He sure as hell never needed them....

Don't make me kick your ass!

He knew that's what Buzz would be saying to him if Buzz was around now. If Buzz saw him staring at that newspaper and wanting to toss it into the pool. There was no way Buzz would have stood for this damn black mood he'd been in since his best friend's death.

Bentley—Buzz—Adams. Like Katie, Tate's fiancée, Tate had known Buzz all his life, despite the fact that they'd come from different backgrounds. Politics and the military—that's where Buzz's roots were. His father, grandfather and great-grandfather had all been high-ranking army officers who each served as military advisors to presidents. But Buzz's own father hadn't wanted his family to live the nomadic military life, so Buzz had been raised at his grandparents' estate, just down the road.

Tate and Buzz had gone to private school together. They'd gone to college together. They'd even gone to medical school together and applied for residency at the same hospital. Their paths hadn't veered until residency was over and Tate had opted for a specialty in surgery while Buzz had followed his family's tradition and joined the army to serve as a doctor overseas.

Going to war was the first thing Tate and Buzz hadn't done together.

If only Buzz hadn't broken his tradition with Tate to follow his family's tradition....

But he had.

And everything else was water under the bridge now.

Everything but this funk Tate couldn't seem to shake.

He knew he was one hell of a downer these days, that everyone was wondering where the old Tate was. Most of the time he was wondering it himself. But the old Tate just didn't seem to be there anymore.

He also knew his lousy mood was going to factor in when the news about his engagement to Katie came out, and he regretted that. He didn't want people saying that Katie had bailed because he wasn't much fun anymore. Katie didn't deserve that.

She hadn't ended their engagement because he couldn't seem to lighten up. She'd made that clear and he didn't doubt it. That just wasn't Katie. In fact, he thought that if he'd put any effort into talking her out of breaking their engagement, the bad mood would have likely kept her around because she would have felt guilty for leaving him at a low point.

But he hadn't put any effort into keeping things going with her. Why should he have when she was right? She'd said that she'd been thinking that maybe long-term friendship and family pressure and the general belief that they'd end up together shouldn't, ultimately, be why they *did* end up together. That she didn't think she had the kind of feelings for him that she should have going into marriage. That she didn't feel passionate about him.

Maybe that should have been insulting, but it hadn't been. Instead, he'd understood it. His own feelings for Katie had never been all-consuming or particularly passionate. Which was probably why calling things off just hadn't mattered a whole lot to him.

Of course, it also didn't really matter to him that Katie wanted to keep the breakup a secret until she could see her parents in Florida and explain it to them.

It didn't matter to him that Katie wasn't head over heels for him.

It didn't matter to him that they'd broken up.

It didn't matter to him that he needed to maintain the pretense that they hadn't.

Since Buzz's death, and even more so in the six months since he'd been back from Baghdad, it had just been tough for things like that—for most of what mattered to the people around him—to have the importance they might have had before....

He took a drink of his coffee and then replaced the cup on the table, staring into the steaming beverage that still remained.

He liked his coffee strong and black, and looking into the brew now made him think of Tanya Kimbrough's eyes. They were the color of Italian espresso—dark, rich, liquid pools of espresso....

Recalling that made him think of one thing that had mattered to him—last night and finding Tanya Kimbrough in the library. That had definitely mattered.

When he'd found her there he'd taken a mental inventory of what he and Blake had said because what was going on with the business *did* matter. He'd recalled that they'd said the jewelry business was in a slump, that they believed they knew where the Santa Magdalena diamond was, that Blake was buying all the canary diamonds to use as a tie-in.

Then there were the papers Tanya had seen on the desk, too—Blake must have forgotten the file and while there hadn't been anything in it but preliminaries for the advertising campaign, it was still information they didn't want released.

And after cataloging what Tanya Kimbrough could have known, the wheels of Tate's mind had started to turn, imagining her prematurely revealing that they were looking for the Santa Magdalena diamond. No, he and Blake hadn't talked about the crucial clue Blake had discovered in the border of the deed to the land and silver mines they'd taken over from the Foleys decades ago. Still, if word leaked that there was a very real reason to suspect the diamond might be found? Any number of treasure hunters could descend on them to complicate the search. And possibly accidentally find the diamond before they did.

Not good.

Tate had considered what would happen if word leaked that Blake was cornering the market on canary diamonds and coming out with a new line of Spanish-influenced designs to coincide with the discovery of the Santa Magdalena. Their competitors would launch lines of their own to steal their thunder and undermine their sales and, potentially, leave Blake at a disadvantage in breathing new life into the business.

Also not good.

And let the world know that the renowned McCord's Jewelers was in a decline? That the family fortunes were compromised?

Certainly not good.

And since Blake was up to his eyeballs in the family's problems already and—as usual—trying to bear the burden as much on his own as he could, rotten mood or not, Tate had decided that it was better if he dealt with the housekeeper's daughter rather than dumping any more on his brother.

Which was why he'd struck that bargain with her for an insider's look at the Mc-Cords and an exclusive on the diamond if they found it. Left to her own devices, Tanya Kimbrough could cause trouble and he was going to do whatever he had to to prevent that. If that meant sticking to her like glue to keep a close eye on her for the time being, then that's what he was going to do.

It's a dirty job, but somebody has to do it....

Tate knew that's what Buzz would be saying to him if he told his friend he was only taking on Tanya Kimbrough to spare Blake.

Yeah, okay, it was hardly as dirty a job as studying a dusty deed or digging around in the dirt of a deserted old silver mine. Keeping an eye on a beautiful woman was definitely not drawing the short straw.

And Tanya *was* a beautiful woman.

The scrawny, funny-looking kid had grown into a knockout—there was no question about that.

Her hair was as dark as her eyes—coffee-nib brown—and so shiny it looked like satin. Coupled with those eyes against a fair, flawless complexion, she'd been the freshest-faced burglar in existence. Fresh-faced and beautiful even without any visible signs of makeup, with that thin nose and those pale pink lips, those high cheekbones and the slightly squarish jawline sweeping up from a chin that looked as if it could be a little sassy.

Unlike her taller, slightly stocky mother, Tanya was petite—no more than five-four he was guessing. She was thin, but not too thin, and she had curves in all the right places—at least he thought she did even though that chopped-up sweatshirt she'd had on had done more camouflaging than revealing.

Of course it *had* revealed one shoulder before she'd yanked the fabric back into place. And the mere sight of that creamy skin had made him suddenly aware of his own heartbeat. And the fact that it had sped up....

Only slightly.

But still, that was more than most things had done to him lately. A simple bare shoulder...

Hell, he was a doctor. He saw naked shoulders—and naked everything else—all the time. Why had a simple glimpse of Tanya Kimbrough's shoulder done anything at all to him?

Maybe it had been an adrenaline rush, he reasoned. He'd just had that argument with

Blake and then spotted someone he'd initially thought to be a stranger lurking behind the desk. He hadn't actually been alarmed, but it wasn't beyond the realm of possibility that his subconscious had set off an alert response. After Baghdad, that seemed likely.

And if it had felt like something other than that?

He was likely only misinterpreting it.

He did know one thing, though—he wasn't hating the idea of keeping an eye on Tanya Kimbrough.

In fact, if he analyzed it, he'd say he might even be looking forward to it.

He might say he'd even gotten a small rush out of that back-and-forth with her last night. A small rush that he wouldn't mind having again…

But that *couldn't* matter, he told himself.

The charge he'd gotten out of their verbal exchange and the fact that she'd held her own with him, the smooth skin on a shoulder he'd been inclined to mold his hand around, the silky hair he'd wanted to see fall free, the lips he'd had a fleeting thought of tasting, the tight little body hidden behind funny-looking pants and a sweatshirt that someone had taken scissors to—none of that was as important as protecting his family, or as important as his promise to Katie to pretend they were still engaged until she told him otherwise.

But still…

He *was* looking forward to seeing the housekeeper's daughter again.

And continuing to see much more of her for a while to keep her contained?

That didn't feel like a hardship either.…

"What are you doing here?"

Tanya could see that Tate was surprised to find her waiting for him when he left the operating suite of Meridian General Hospital at eight o'clock Saturday night.

"I told you you were going to talk to me whether you liked it or not," she countered heatedly.

"When did you tell me that?"

"At the end of the sixteenth voice mail I left you today."

"I got called in for an emergency surgery early this morning. I've been standing at an operating table for the last—" he glanced at a clock on the wall "—eleven hours and twenty minutes. Not a lot of message checking goes on when I'm up to my elbows in a man's gut."

"Gross," Tanya said reflexively.

Tate merely raised an eyebrow at that, giving her the impression that that was the response he'd been going for.

But if he thought disgusting her was going to make her back down, he needed to think again.

"Eleven hours and twenty minutes of surgery or not, we're going to talk," she insisted.

"If I've inspired sixteen voice mails I guess we'll have to," he said sardonically but sounding weary nonetheless. "First I have to let the family know how my patient is—" he nodded in the direction of a group of people she hadn't noticed before but now realized were also waiting for him "—then I have to write orders to get this guy into recovery. After that my plan is for a quick bite to eat at the deli across the street before I have to operate on the other passenger from this car accident. So if you're determined that we talk right now, you can either wait for me here and go over to the deli with me, or go ahead of me to the deli—but one way or another there's only going to be a small

window before my next patient is prepped
and ready to be opened up."

It irked Tanya all the more to have him dic-
tate to her, but she wouldn't let that stop her.

"Fine, I'll wait here," she said cuttingly.

Now that she'd finally found him, she had
no intention of letting him slip away from
her. After calling his cell phone all day,
she'd questioned almost the entire house
staff before finding someone who knew Tate
was at the hospital. When she'd called the
hospital she'd been told she couldn't speak
to him because he was in surgery. That had
prompted her to come here to ambush him
as soon as he got out. But she'd been lying
in wait for nearly two hours and was not
willing to go ahead of him to the deli and
risk him not showing up.

So she perched on the edge of the same
seat she'd occupied for the last two hours
and watched him intently.

When he was finished talking to his patient's family, they headed for the elevators
and Tate moved to the nurses' station. He
said something to the nurse there and while
she went to do his bidding, Tanya continued
to keep him in her sights.

As she did, it occurred to her that while,

over the years, she'd seen Tate McCord in tennis whites, in tuxedos, in suits and ties and casual clothes of all kinds, she'd never seen him in scrubs. And that he looked too sexy to believe in the loose-fitting, teal blue cotton garments that resembled pajamas more than street clothing.

Then, adding to that sexiness he seemed unconscious of, he rolled his shoulders, arched his spine and raised his elbows to shoulder height to pull his arms back until even Tanya heard something crack—obviously working out the kinks that hours of surgery had left.

But regardless of the fact that she was overly aware of every little thing about him, she refused to let any of it influence her. She was steaming mad and she was going to let him know it. Nothing—including being one of the best-looking, sexiest men she'd ever seen—gave him license to mess with her career! Not even if she had overstepped her bounds the previous night.

The nurse brought him a metal clipboard then, and when he was done writing the orders for his patient, he handed the chart back to the nurse and finally turned to Tanya.

"Ready?"

"You don't need to change clothes?" she asked, hoping he would and that different clothes might help lessen the effect he was having on her in scrubs.

But he shook his head. "Hadn't planned on it. Like I said, I have another surgery scheduled tonight and the deli doesn't have a dress code. Unless it offends you in some way…"

"I couldn't care less what you're wearing," she lied.

"Then let's go get something to eat before I pass out from hunger."

The trip through the hospital and across the street was filled with Tate greeting and exchanging quips with nurses, attendants, volunteers, other doctors and even the janitor. Then they reached the deli and he was right—there were more customers dressed the way he was than in anything that resembled the slacks and shirt Tanya was wearing.

Not that she felt out of place, but it did occur to her as she peered at the other men in scrubs that she didn't find any of *them* particularly attractive….

Still, she did everything she could to overlook Tate's appeal as he ordered his "usual." She rejected his offer of food and accepted only a lemonade before they went to one of the booths that lined the walls of the small restaurant.

Despite what he'd said, Tate seemed more tired than hungry. After setting his pastrami sandwich and iced tea on the table, he left them untouched while he sat lengthwise on his side of the booth to put his feet up. He also rested his head against the wall and closed his eyes—probably to wind down and relax the way he'd intended to do without her company.

But Tanya wasn't going to be ignored.

"So how did you have time to ruin my life if you were up to your elbows in someone's insides all day and most of tonight?" she demanded before she'd even sipped her lemonade.

Rather than add to Tate's stress, that actually brought an indication of amusement in a slight upward curl of the corners of his mouth even before he opened his eyes to look at her. "How did I *ruin* your life?"

"I got a call at nine o'clock this morning from the owner of WDGN—not the station manager who hired me, but the station *owner*—"

"Chad Burton."

"Your friend," Tanya said derisively.

"We're more acquaintances than close friends. I went through school with his son, Chad Junior. I helped Junior pass chemistry and physics, although he ended up an interior decorator, not a doctor the way Chad Senior had hoped. But Chad Senior has always been grateful. Chad Senior and I have also been on a lot of committees together, we play golf now and then—"

"You're friends enough to have called him sometime between last night and nine o'clock this morning to persuade him to put me on a leave of absence—"

"With pay," Tate pointed out, not bothering to pretend he hadn't been behind today's turn of events.

"With or without pay, from today forward—indefinitely—I'm on special assignment to work the McCord story. That means no on-air time, no other duties, no other stories, no other assignments, no chance to prove myself in any other way or gain any other ground after just two weeks of working there. I was told I'm not to show my face at the station until I have the whole McCord thing ready to be put together."

"But you're still on the payroll, so—"

"This isn't about money!" Tanya said, ferociously whispering to keep from shouting. "If I don't go back with something good—like the discovery of the Santa Magdalena diamond itself—I'll be *lucky* to be doing the agriculture reports on the predawn weekend newscasts. Plus they'll probably hire someone else to do my job in the meantime and that someone else could just replace me if the McCords don't come up with the diamond and all I have is a human-interest piece. You may have put in a good word for me to get this job, but my credentials and abilities actually got it for me, and you don't have the right to pull it out from under me just to suit your purposes!"

He sat up straight in the booth, putting his feet on the floor and finally unwrapping his sandwich to take a bite. Not until he'd chewed, swallowed and washed it down with a drink of his iced tea, did he say, "I had to make sure you didn't have the opportunity to go back on your word to keep quiet."

"I could still do that—I could go to a Foley-owned station."

He remained unruffled by her threat. "You could," he said. "But that talk about loyalty last night got me to thinking—your mom has worked for us for twenty-two years. She oversees the whole staff. She's my mom's right hand around the house. I'm not going to say we're all family, but there's a connection that you sure as hell don't have with our archrivals. You must feel *some* amount of loyalty."

"How much loyalty did you feel when you called Chad Burton?"

"Today or when I called him to say I was sending over your résumé?"

Tanya glared at him. "That was something my mother did without telling me until *after* it was done because she wanted me to move back here. The résumé you sent over wasn't even a recent one. It was the first one I did out of college—my mother found it in an old file. *I* faxed them the *real,* current résumé, which is what got me the interview."

Tate ignored all of that and merely went on to answer her question about his loyalty.

"I wasn't being disloyal. I was only playing it safe. And Chad was thrilled with the idea of getting an insider's view of the Mc-Cords. Plus, even though I didn't do anything but allude to the diamond, I let him know that there was the potential for big news to come along with the *human-interest* stuff, and he was nearly drooling over the chance for WDGN to be the one to break that big news. This really could put you on the map."

"I lose ground not being there, not having my face in front of a camera every chance I can get," she insisted. "There's no reason I couldn't still be doing my job there and compiling the McCord information."

"But now you don't have to do anything but focus on the McCords."

"Who are *not* the center of the universe, just in case you were wondering!" Tanya said, her voice raised enough to garner a glance from the couple at the nearest table.

"It's just a precaution," Tate said calmly.

"You're trying to control me," Tanya accused.

"Yes, I am. But only in this and only for the sake of the greater good."

"As if that makes it all right."

"Was it all right that you broke into my family's home last night to spy on us and try to get information to expose things that could hurt us if they got out at the wrong time?" he reasoned.

"So you're exacting revenge?"

"Nooo, not at all. You still have your job and your paycheck. You have the chance to do an exclusive story on the McCords and be the reporter who tells the world if we find the Santa Magdalena diamond. You just won't be doing anything *but* that for now."

Tanya narrowed her eyes at him. "You'd better give me a good story," she warned.

"And you'd better put all your energy into me and *getting* a good story," he countered.

"Into *you?* Why would I put my energy into *you?*"

He smiled. A slow, lazy, sexy smile. "I guess because I'm the teller-of-the-tale, and the happier I am, the better the tale-telling?"

"And what does that mean? That not only do I have to climb the mountain to get the answers from The Great One, but that I have to bring enticements, too?" she asked facetiously.

His smile stretched into a grin and he didn't at all look like the sad, somber, lackluster shadow of his former self that her mother and the rest of the staff described him as.

"Enticements?" he repeated as if he hadn't been thinking that until she suggested it. "I like the sound of that."

"Well, get over it," she advised bluntly, knowing he was merely having some fun at her expense. "There's no way I'm bringing *enticements* to get you to tell me about your family."

"Too bad," he pretended to lament.

"I'm serious, Tate," she said, using his name for the first time as an adult.

"Yes, you are, Tanya," he agreed, barely suppressing a smile. "You are *very* serious."

"I mean it—you'd better give me something good enough to make this *sabbatical* worth my while."

He seemed to take that in a different—and lascivious—vein than how she'd intended it because his smile appeared full force again and it was laced with wicked amusement.

But before he said anything else, the pager clipped to the bottom of his shirt went off, drawing his attention.

He glanced down at it. "I have to get back," he announced, grabbing another quick bite of his only half-eaten sandwich and then rewrapping the rest to take with him.

As he did, he returned to what they'd been talking about. "All I meant when I said that you should put your energy into me was into *spending time* with me to get your story—as part of the job you really are still doing."

He stood, guzzled most of his iced tea and, after replacing the glass on the table, added, "And to that end, why don't we start with a real dinner tomorrow night? My treat and we can both eat."

"Since it's now my *job,* I guess so," Tanya conceded.

"Eight o'clock? I'll meet you at the pool and we'll go somewhere from there?"

Tanya nodded and that was all it took to send him rushing out of the deli.

As she watched him go her anger at him began to waver. Maybe it was the sight of him from behind in those scrubs that loosely covered his broad shoulders and barely grazed a derriere to die for.

But instead of thinking about the influence he'd used to keep her under his thumb, she was thinking more about the fact that her job now was essentially spending time with Tate McCord.

And how, as much as she should be resenting that, she was actually a little excited by the prospect....

Chapter Three

"I don't like it, Tanya. And I don't think it's a good idea."

"It'll be fine, JoBeth."

Calling her mother by name and in the special teasing, cajoling tone Tanya used usually made her mother laugh. Now it barely elicited a smile.

When Tanya hadn't gone in to do the early Sunday newscast, JoBeth had asked why. Tanya had had to tell her mother what was going on with Tate and the special assignment to do the McCord story—although she'd omitted the fact that it was the result of being caught snooping in the library on Friday night.

"The McCords have always been good to us, Tanya. When your father walked out and left me with a two-year-old and no money and no education and no skills, Mrs. McCord—"

"—not only gave you a job, but since the housekeeper at the time wasn't living here, she let us live in this bungalow when none of the other maids got that kind of accommodation," Tanya said, repeating what her mother had said many times as she'd grown up. Then she continued with what she knew JoBeth was going to say. "Mrs. McCord promoted you from maid to housekeeper to overseeing the whole staff. She gave you flexible hours whenever I was sick or you wanted to go to my school meetings and functions. She wrote my recommendation letter to college and to the scholarship committee that paid my tuition for four years. I haven't forgotten any of that."

"But now you'll try to dig up dirt on the McCords to get yourself more on-air time? That's not right."

They were at the kitchen table with coffee and toast, both of them in their bathrobes, not long out of bed. JoBeth had Sunday mornings off and Tanya regretted that rather than relaxing, her mother was stressed about this.

"I'm not going to *dig up dirt*," she assured JoBeth, deciding to put a positive spin on the turn of events to ease her mother's mind. "Some of this even came at the *suggestion* of Tate, who also talked to the station owner— that's why I won't be doing anything but devoting myself to this for a while. Tate is going to be walking me through the family history, including the reasons why there's a problem with anyone named Foley—which I've never understood. Hopefully, he'll let me have an insider's look that will include finding the Santa Magdalena diamond—if they actually do—and it will all give me a leg up here in Dallas. So really, this is still a lot like the little extra help Mrs. McCord has given along the way—think of it like that."

But apparently Tanya's mother was not won over by that argument because JoBeth narrowed her dark eyes at Tanya, increasing the lines that fanned out from their corners. "These people are my *employers,* Tanya. I'm dependent on them for my *livelihood.* For my whole day-to-day existence."

"And I'm not going to do anything to

jeopardize that." If what she'd done Friday night didn't count...

But suddenly Tanya took stock of JoBeth sitting across from her at the tiny table they'd eaten most of their meals on.

Her mother worked long hours that had aged her—something Tanya saw in the single shock of prematurely white hair at JoBeth's temple. But Tanya knew that her mother was not only grateful for the job, JoBeth enjoyed it and the camaraderie and closeness of the household staff that went with it.

And if that hair that was down now would soon be in a bun that was as tightly wound as her mother had always had to be, that control was something Tanya knew her mother took pride in. If the milkiness of JoBeth's skin was evidence that vacation sun rarely touched it, it wasn't for want of time off, it was because JoBeth preferred her routine here to sitting on a Caribbean beach. If JoBeth's slight pudginess came from caring for the McCords rather than paying attention to exercise or cautious eating for herself, Tanya knew that her mother would say it was a treat to get to taste the delicacies prepared by the McCords' chef.

And Tanya was also well aware of the fact that while the cottage with its two small bedrooms and this area that combined kitchen and living room was hardly luxury living, her mother loved the housekeeper's bungalow and considered it her home—a home she'd refused to leave even when Tanya had tried to persuade her to move to California with her.

Which all added up to more than a livelihood that JoBeth didn't want to lose, it was the life her mother had made for herself. And Tanya realized even more than she had before that she had to be careful not to do anything that would compromise that or put it at risk.

"Who better to do this story?" she said to her mother then. "I'm obligated to report on any skeletons I might find in the McCord closets, but I won't sensationalize them. I'll do a fair and honest piece that will come primarily from information Tate relays—so you know there aren't going to *be* a lot of negatives in the mix—and I won't go searching for them the way someone else might. I'll take what Tate gives, hope it all leads to the bigger story of the discovery of the diamond and leave it at that."

"Tate," her mother echoed. "You shouldn't be imposing on him. He has too much on his mind as it is. Since his friend died in Iraq, since he came back from there himself, he's troubled, Tanya. You can't be bothering him to get yourself—"

"He offered, Mama. I won't be *bothering* him."

"He offered?" JoBeth parroted ominously.

"He volunteered," Tanya amended because she'd caught the sudden switch in her mother's concerns. Now it wasn't the McCords who JoBeth was worried about, it was Tanya. And that was a more fierce protectiveness.

"You're a beautiful girl, Tanya—"

"Says my mother." Tanya dismissed the compliment.

"Tate has eyes."

"And a fiancée," Tanya reminded. Then, in an attempt to calm her mother's fears, she said, "Tate is *engaged* to Katie Whitcomb-Salgar—the person he's been promised to since they played together in the sandbox. And it wouldn't matter even if they hadn't finally gotten engaged—I know better than to get involved with Tate McCord, of all people. This is strictly business. For both of us. He's going to walk me through some family history and give me the exclusive on the outcome of whatever it is that's going on with the Santa Magdalena diamond—that's all there is to it. There's nothing personal in it for either of us."

"For your own sake, you'd better make sure of that," JoBeth said, her round face reflecting the fact that Tanya had failed to ease her mind. "I don't want you getting hurt."

"I won't get hurt, Mama. I told you, it's strictly business."

JoBeth stared at her for a long moment as if she were hoping to be able to see the future in Tanya's face. Then, with no indication of whether or not she thought she had, she took her obvious concerns and her crossword puzzle into the living room.

Tanya interpreted that as a sign that her mother was tentatively accepting what she'd told her.

But while she stayed where she was at the kitchen table to finish her breakfast, Tanya was still thinking about it all.

This *was* strictly business between her and Tate—she hadn't said that simply to appease JoBeth. Tanya had outgrown wanting to be a McCord a long time ago. Yes, as a very young, starry-eyed girl she'd fantasized about being a part of what went on at the big house. But as soon as her mother had realized that was what she was doing, JoBeth had taken measures to keep Tanya's feet firmly planted on the ground. And ultimately—eventually—Tanya had come to see for herself that the McCords' life was not a life she wanted.

Of course mountains of money would be nice, but other than that? The McCords were under constant scrutiny, their every movement watched. They were talked about and criticized, envied and resented. And none of that appealed to Tanya.

Plus, the McCords existed in an insular world where everything remained the same from generation to generation. Where the names, the faces, the cliques never changed. Where new blood was seldom let in. Where some fight, started long, long ago for reasons Tanya wasn't sure even they knew, was still burning. It all just seemed so stagnant to her.

And in keeping with that, Tate *was* engaged to Katie Whitcomb-Salgar—the daughter of his mother's and late father's close friends and someone who had moved within that same small, insulated circle his entire life, too.

But Tanya understood why the fact that Tate was engaged didn't put her mother's mind to rest. Both Tanya and JoBeth had been around the McCords long enough to know that the relationship between Tate and Katie ran a pattern—together, not together, together again.

Just because they'd finally gotten formally engaged didn't mean this was the time they made it to the altar. One or the other of them could still decide to put the wedding off, to separate the way they had dozens of times in the past.

And if that happened and Tanya caught Tate's attention during the interim? He could be very persuasive. But in the end Tanya would only be a dalliance for Tate before he went back to Katie anyway. Which he always did.

That was what Tanya knew her mother was worried about.

But JoBeth didn't need to be. Not only would Tanya never knowingly get involved with anyone who was already involved with someone else, there was no way she would allow herself to be one of Tate McCord's fleeting detours from the woman his family had chosen for him.

No, the whole thing—what it meant to be a McCord and interrupting Tate's destiny to be with Katie Whitcomb-Salgar—was just not for Tanya.

Regardless of how terrific Tate might have looked in those scrubs last night.

But he *had* looked terrific....

Still, after a moment's indulgence in that mental image, Tanya shoved it aside.

That man was off-off-off-limits, as far as she was concerned. The only purpose he served was to provide her with a good story that she could use to boost her standing at the station and launch her career in Dallas.

And the fact that he was the drop-dead gorgeous, charming, smart, accomplished Tate McCord was merely something she needed to overlook in order to keep a professional and personal distance.

Which she had every intention of doing.

"Dinner with you meant the country club—I suppose I should have guessed, but I was thinking we were going somewhere low-key where we could get down to business," Tanya said as they left the club's fine-dining—and fanciest—restaurant.

The valet had Tate's sports car waiting for them. Tate went around to the driver's side. One valet opened the passenger door for Tanya, while another opened the driver's door for Tate. Only as their doors were closed for them and they were both fastening their seat belts did Tate say, "I can *get down to business,* if that's what you want. I just thought we were having a friendly dinner," he said with an innuendo-laden tone that purposely misinterpreted her words.

"What I want is to get down to the *business* I'm being paid to do—a profile on you and your family," she qualified, not taking his slightly flirtatious bait but also making sure her tone was amiable. There had been confrontation between them on the last two nights and that was not a pattern she wanted to set.

Tate pulled out of the wrought-iron gates of the country club and into traffic without responding.

"Nothing work related was accomplished at all," Tanya continued anyway. "You ended up talking more to your cronies than giving me any useful information about the McCords."

"My *cronies?*" Tate repeated as he headed for his family's estate.

"The rest of the country-club set. Or was that the purpose of dinner at the club—to avoid doing what you agreed to do and at the same time show me that the McCords hobnob with Dallas's richest, most famous, most powerful and influential? And how even among the richest, most famous, powerful and influential, it was still you who was catered to to the point of the bartender counting the number of ice cubes he put in your predinner private reserve scotch?"

"Would I do something like that?" he said with no inflection at all, leaving her clueless as to whether or not that had been his motive.

"And for future reference," she went on, still conversationally, "you should warn the person you're bringing to the country club ahead of time. I was the only woman not in pearls." In fact, she'd been underdressed in a pair of linen slacks and simple camp shirt, while Tate was dressed more appropriately in a cocoa-colored suit with an off-white shirt and brown tie.

"Pearls are not mandatory," he informed her as they gained distance from the private club where memberships were primarily inherited and only the first names on the roster varied from decade to decade.

Tate took his eyes off the road to glance at her, his expression showing a hint of curiosity now. "So let me see if I have this straight—you're mad because we just had a nice dinner?"

"I'm not *mad,*" she insisted. And she wasn't. "The food was fantastic and the waitstaff treated me like a queen." And in between the avalanche of obligatory hellos and small talk that had demanded Tate's attention while Tanya was barely given dismissive nods after her introductions, he'd been a perfectly pleasant dinner companion. "But I thought tonight would be the kickoff to my collecting information—or else why should we be together? And it's frustrating that nothing along those lines got done."

And as a result, she hadn't had work to keep her from noticing how easy it was to be with Tate.

"I don't need to see what a hotshot you are," she added.

"Ouch! Hotshot? That sounds bad."

"I'm just saying that the country-club side of you and of your family is not news. That kind of thing is in the society columns every day. You promised me the private side and that's not what tonight was."

"What tonight was," Tate said as they neared home, "was to make amends for costing you your on-air time and leaving you hanging yesterday. It's also Sunday and the club's regular chef takes Sundays off. His understudy—or whatever the guy who fills in for him is called—takes over in the kitchen on Sundays and the understudy goes all out to show his stuff when he gets that chance. I like to see what he comes up with. It's usually different and innovative and interesting. Like tonight—thin slices of Kobe beef that we cooked ourselves over a hot rock—so country club or not, why shouldn't we have gone there for dinner? Pearls notwithstanding?"

"Because that's all this turned out to be—a nice dinner—"

"And that's a crime?"

"I'm with you to do an assignment, not to go on a date," she said reasonably.

"This wasn't a date, it was just dinner," he said.

Which was part of what she knew she needed to guard against—what seemed like a really great date to her was nothing but an ordinary, everyday dinner to him....

"Or is that how this has to be?" he went on. "Strictly business? Do we need to sit on opposite sides of a desk, only between nine and five, and be formal and stuffy?"

Strictly business—that's what she'd told her mother this was. That was what she wanted it to be, what she needed it to be. But stuffy and formal? Sitting on opposite sides of a desk? Not only was that unlikely to get her the same kind of intimate portrait that came when an interviewee was relaxed and talking freely, but it definitely didn't appeal to her when it came to Tate McCord.

And that was another warning sign—the fact that Tate was striking a personal note in her that had nothing to do with work.

On the other hand, her first priority *was* getting the best story she could, and to that end, friendly and casual was the route to take.

"No, I don't want this to be done sitting opposite each other at a desk," she answered his question a little belatedly. "But I want to see the side of the McCords that isn't about being greeted by name by a state senator or where everyone in the place knows what you eat and drink—like tonight and last night, too. I'm well aware of the fact that the McCords are Texas royalty—even walking through the hospital with you was like being in a parade. What I'm hoping is that there's *something* else to you all. Something that gets you outside of your comfort zone and puts you in touch with the rest of the world—you know, those of us who are real?"

They'd reached the McCord estate but Tate hadn't pulled up to the garages. He'd gone around the other way to stop as near to the housekeeper's bungalow as he could get. When he turned off the engine he angled in his seat to look at Tanya.

"And just how far outside of your *comfort zone* have you ventured? How in touch with the rest of the world are you—as a *real* person? Because *worldly* is not how you strike me at the ripe old age of…what? Twenty-three?"

He was apparently not opposed to more confrontation tonight.

"Okay, I'm not *worldly,*" Tanya agreed. "But I think there's a huge portion of our society and the everyday life that most people live that you *are* out of touch with," she said, still calm but pulling no punches.

"*I'm* out of touch?" Tate said as if he were challenging her. But at the same time, something about this debate also seemed to have amused him because his eyes were bright and alive and he was barely suppressing a smile.

And as long as she wasn't alienating him, she didn't back down. "If you're talking about having gone to the Middle East like I've been told that you did, then no, that isn't an experience I've had or can relate to. And while I don't know why you went or where you were or how close to the war you got, or anything but that you spent a year somewhere over there, what I'm thinking is that you don't even have a concept of what life is like for the everyday person *here*, outside of your cushy existence. Given that, it's no wonder that what you must have encountered there was difficult for you to handle, and maybe if you hadn't been wrapped in cotton before—"

Tanya stopped herself because she realized suddenly that she was talking out of school. She was only guessing at what was going on with him, guessing that the reason he was so affected by his year away was because he'd gone from a virtual cocoon into something his life—of all lives—hadn't prepared him for. And she was doing that guessing based solely on what she'd heard from her mother and the other house staff.

"I'm sorry, that was out of line," she apologized in a hurry. "It's just that there's a lot of talk about you being depressed and changed and—"

She was getting in deeper and deeper.

"I should shut up," she concluded.

"And you think that because I spent my life *wrapped in cotton* that seeing what I saw in Iraq was more than I could take?"

Oh, she was sooo far over the line....

"I'm not even sure how we got into this so let's back up. Even when I lived here as a kid what I saw was more the trappings of your family's money and status and what it allowed you all. But that isn't the story I want. Or the story I thought you agreed to give me. Whatever is going on with you—in your head—is your own business and none of mine. I shouldn't have shot off my mouth about it."

"But that's what everybody in your circle is saying? That I'm depressed?"

She wanted to kick herself. She also didn't

want to get anyone into trouble and knew she had to do some damage control.

"Whether you realize it or not, people like my mom and some of the other staff who have been around a long time care about you. They're worried about you. They're only saying that you seem to have a lot on your mind, and my mom—in particular—doesn't like that I'm bothering you when you don't seem to be yourself. It's not like you're being gossiped about."

He stared at her for a long moment and beyond the fact that he still appeared entertained by her discomfort, she couldn't tell what he was thinking.

Then he said, "You can reassure everyone that I'm not depressed and that they don't need to worry."

"Good to know," Tanya said, not feeling at all relieved.

She was hoping for more from him that might let her know he wasn't going to make a big deal about this with the staff but there was no more to come.

Instead Tate pivoted in his seat again and got out, coming around to her side. But it seemed strange to wait for him to open her door. This *wasn't* a date, after all.

It also felt odd to have him walk her through the tree-lined path that led to her mother's cottage but that was what he did.

"Is living with your mom again a permanent arrangement?" he asked along the way, apparently returning to small talk.

"No, I'm just staying with her until I recoup some of my moving expenses and can find a place of my own."

"Do you have paper and something to write with?" he asked as they came through the trees on the other side and stepped onto the bungalow's front stoop.

Tanya didn't know what he was getting at, but she opened the small purse she was carrying and handed him a pen and a notepad she'd brought with her thinking that she was going to be working tonight.

He wrote an address on the paper and handed it back to her. Tanya assumed it was a lead on an apartment.

"Meet me there tomorrow morning at nine," he commanded.

Tanya looked from the paper to him, trying not to notice that the porch light illuminated the high spots of his handsome face and threw the hollows and angles into sharp

shadows that only made him look dangerously attractive.

"I really won't be able to afford an apartment for a couple of months so it would be
a waste of time—"

"It isn't an apartment."

"Oh. Then where am I going?" she asked.

"You'll see when you get there. No pearls.
Come comfortable and ready to dig in."

"Shall I bring a shovel?" she joked.

"No pearls, no shovel," he answered but
he obviously wanted to be mysterious and
wasn't going to give her any other details.

"Oka-ay," she muttered. Then, rather than
pursue a subject he wasn't going to expand
on, she said, "Thanks for dinner."

That made him chuckle. "Even though it
wasn't what you had in mind?"

"The food was still great. You're right, the
understudy chef does do interesting things."

"Maybe next Sunday I'll just see if he'll
do them takeout so we can avoid the dreaded
country club," Tate said wryly, making
Tanya smile this time.

"Wow, you can do that," he mock mar-
veled.

"What?"

"Smile. I was beginning to wonder. And

it's nice, too. Who would have thought Miss Serious had a nice smile...."

"Miss Serious?"

"Well, there was nothing lighthearted about catching you in the library. You took me to task last night over stepping in with the news station. And tonight you've been all business even when business wasn't going on, and then you took me to task again on the way home. Plus you said yourself last night that you're serious—"

"That was a figure of speech. What I said was that I was serious about getting a substantial story out of this."

"Still, you're just plain serious, as far as I've seen. Maybe your mom and her cohorts should be worrying more about you than me."

Okay, so there hadn't been a whole lot of levity to any of the times they'd encountered each other since Friday night.

"This *is* business for me," she reminded him.

He smiled again, a pleased, warm smile that she liked entirely too much. "I'm glad you said business and not work. I don't think I like being *work* for anyone."

"Just make sure *business* gets done from here on," she pretended to chastise.

"Tomorrow, 9:00 a.m.," he countered.

She wondered if she was going to arrive at the address on the paper and find him sitting behind a desk. And if she would be expected to spend from then until five o'clock on the opposite side of that desk taking dictation on the story of his life.

She wouldn't put it past him.

But she knew better than to try to get any more information out of him about that, so she merely said, "Tomorrow, 9:00 a.m."

That seemed to satisfy him. It showed in his smile as he went on peering into her face for a moment more before he said, "You can tell your mother that you aren't."

"That I aren't what?"

He laughed. "That is some really rotten grammar for a journalist."

"That I'm *not* what?" she corrected the mistake she'd made on purpose, trying not to bask in the sound of his laugh or the fact that she'd inspired it.

"You're not bothering me. In fact, you're kind of a little spitfire and I'm getting a kick out of it."

"*Little spitfire?* You're aware that that's

very condescending, aren't you?" she said even though it gave her a tiny rush to hear that she was rousing something in him.

"Hey, I'm just a sheltered, pampered, out-of-touch rich boy, what do I know?" he joked.

Again Tanya smiled, adding a hint of a laugh to it. And maybe her lighter side really was a novelty to him because several minutes lapsed while Tate just seemed to study her as if he couldn't quite figure her out.

Several minutes that made something else flash through Tanya's mind—that people in this position, saying good-night at the door after having spent an evening together and sharing a nice dinner, very often kissed....

Which of course was not going to happen, she told herself in no uncertain terms.

And it didn't. Because then Tate said, "I'll see you at nine," and turned to retrace his steps to his car.

Tanya watched his retreating back, giving herself a silent but stern talking-to as she did.

There could not ever—*ever*—be thoughts of kissing when it came to Tate McCord.

That was absolutely, positively *un*thinkable.

Unthinkable and undoable.

Absolutely. Positively.

And if she was still standing there even after he was out of sight, even after she could hear his car engine restart, even after she'd heard him drive away?

It was because she was still silently lecturing herself about how she also—absolutely, positively—shouldn't be wondering what it would be like to kiss the mighty Tate McCord, either....

Chapter Four

"Rosa, this is Tanya Kimbrough. Tanya, this is Rosa Marsh—Rosa pretty much runs this place. Rosa, Tanya is going to pitch in for us today as a volunteer. I know you can use her," Tate said as he introduced Tanya to the heavyset nurse.

Then he leaned in close enough to Tanya's ear to whisper so only she could hear, "I thought I'd give you the chance to see how one McCord spends Mondays. And since *you're* so in touch with the *real* people, I figured you'd probably want to do more than just follow me around and take notes."

Tanya could tell that Tate was enjoying

this—there was pure satisfaction on his handsome face as he left her to the woman named Rosa.

When Tanya had arrived at the address Tate had written in her notepad she definitely hadn't found a lead on an apartment for rent. She'd found a surgical clinic for the underprivileged in an extremely neglected portion of Dallas.

She'd also discovered that Tate was known there as Dr. Tate and that if anyone realized he was a McCord, it wasn't an issue. He was just Dr. Tate.

And Tanya was a volunteer for the day.

She didn't mind. It allowed her to watch him in action and pitching in was something she'd been taught to do even as a child. So Tanya followed Rosa's instructions and went to work herself.

She primarily did the nurses' bidding, performing cleanup and making sure patients were comfortable.

The small, inner-city facility was nothing at all like Meridian General Hospital. Sanitary conditions were met but that was about the best that could be said of it. Equipment was old, linens were clean but ragged, the linoleum floor was worn down to the cement beneath it in several places and watermarks decorated the walls and ceiling.

Tanya would never have imagined Tate practicing there. Or fitting in with the two physicians' assistants and four nurses, who were all earthy, outspoken and irreverent. But there wasn't a single indication in anything she saw that made her think he held himself above any of them and they made it clear to her even when he wasn't around that they liked and respected him, and that they felt lucky to work with a surgeon of his caliber.

And the patients—some of them homeless, almost all of them lacking insurance or the ability to pay, many not English-speaking— were nothing like the majority of patients at Meridian General either.

Yet never did she see Tate treat any one of them without respect or compassion.

Plus it wasn't only their outpatient surgical needs—or even their general health needs—he met. He also seemed genuinely concerned for their well-being once they went beyond the peeling walls of the clinic. Numerous times Tanya overheard him ask if the patient had a home in which to recuperate. She saw him slip money to more than a few who clearly needed it. He even took the time to make phone calls to get additional assistance for two patients before he would release them.

She saw him go the extra mile over and over again, but not once did she have the sense that his actions were due to the fact that she was watching, or just to make himself look good. Most of the time he didn't even know she was anywhere near, and there were several instances when she learned what good deed he'd done through the nurses talking to each other. She also saw the nurses take many patients' nonmedical problems to him as if it were a common occurrence for them to enlist him, as if they knew from long before Monday that he was the person to go to.

By the end of the day Tanya wasn't ready to paint him as a saint—with people who weren't under his care he could be demanding and dictatorial. He could be outspoken about any slipups or oversights, and curt with patients' friends or family members who rubbed him wrong. But she had to admit that he wasn't what she'd expected. Or anything like what she'd known of him before. The image she'd had of him as she'd grown up on the peripheries of his life was suddenly altered.

Which didn't help her personally.

Because while finding him awesomely sexy in scrubs was one thing, being impressed by him, discovering that he might actually have some substance, some character, some depth, was much more of a bump in the road for her. It made him more the kind of man she liked, which also made him attractive to her on a whole other level.

Just when she didn't want him to be attractive to her at all...

The last patient wasn't ready to leave the clinic until nearly eight o'clock that night. Then the staff closed up and they all went out together.

Tate made sure his female coworkers got to their cars safely in the unsavory neighborhood. Once he had, he walked Tanya to hers.

"What do you say we meet at the guesthouse in an hour and I pay you for your services today with a little dinner?" he said as they reached her sedan.

It had been a long day and Tanya was tired, but that simple suggestion was enough to wipe it all away. Which she knew was a warning sign and yet she still said, "Dinner?"

"I'm thinking something quick and easy thrown into my wok after I shower. Are you up for it?"

Tate McCord owned a wok and knew how to use it?

"I can't believe you cook, so I guess I should see it for myself."

"Great. Be there in an hour, then," he ordered, opening her car door, waiting for her to get in then closing it.

Recalling her manners slightly late, Tanya started the engine in order to roll down her window and call to him as he went to his own car, "Can I bring anything?"

"Only yourself," he called back.

His tone, his attitude, were nothing but friendly. Completely aboveboard. There wasn't even the vaguest insinuation of anything else. So it was okay for her to have agreed to have dinner with him again, Tanya told herself as she rolled her window up.

And it was, after all, only for the sake of her story. Only to get to know him better— especially now that she'd learned there was more to know than she'd thought before.

And if she was instantly looking forward

to what remained of this evening in a way she hadn't been until then?

It wasn't about the man. It was about the work and getting to the root of the McCords by getting to the root of Tate.

And maybe if she chanted that through the entire drive home, it might start to be true....

At the stroke of nine Tanya was knocking on the door to the guesthouse.

She'd showered. She'd shampooed the antiseptic smell out of her hair. She'd changed into a pair of white cotton pull-on pants and a peach-colored cap-sleeved T-shirt, scrunched her hair into waves and applied some blush, mascara and lip gloss to improve upon the haggard way she'd thought she looked when she'd arrived home.

But not because of Tate. Just because she'd wanted to. Or so she'd insisted both to herself and to her mother when JoBeth had voiced her concerns about another dinner with Tate and the fact that Tanya was primping for it.

"Right on time," Tate announced when he opened the door in answer to her knock.

She could tell that he'd showered, too.

His hair was still slightly damp, the stubble that had shadowed his face when they'd left the clinic was gone and he smelled of a clean, fresh mountain-air cologne that Tanya couldn't resist breathing deeply of because the scent was too enticing.

He'd changed from his scrubs into a plain white T-shirt and a pair of jeans Tanya knew her mother—and his—would consider ready for the ragbag because they were frayed and faded. But even so they looked fabulous on him, riding low on his hips and hugging his rear end like a dream.

And you have no business looking at his rear end! she reprimanded herself as she followed him into the guesthouse in response to his invitation to come in.

"There's wine opened near the fridge over there," he informed her with a nod in that direction as he went straight to the island counter, obviously returning to what he'd been doing before her arrival—cutting vegetables.

And once more Tanya recognized the purely friendly overture that didn't smack of anything inappropriate or the slightest bit flirtatious.

Which was good. If they both stuck with that everything would be fine....

She glanced around at the guesthouse
that was about the same size as her mother's bungalow and arranged the same way—
the small kitchen space and living area were
one wide open room divided by the island
of cupboards with the granite countertop
where Tate prepared their food. The place
was equally as nice as her mother's cottage
but no nicer and it seemed odd for Tate to
be staying there when he had space of his
own in the luxurious main house.

"So, you're living out here?" she fished as
she poured herself a glass of wine and then
joined him at the island counter.

"I have been for the last few months, yes,"
he confirmed.

"Why?" she asked bluntly since he hadn't
offered more information.

He smiled a mystery-man smile and
shrugged without taking his eyes off the
peppers he was expertly slicing into strips.
"Hard to explain," he said. "I suppose the
easiest answer is that I'm not sleeping really
well these days. I do a lot of getting up and
walking around, trying to go back to sleep,
getting up and walking around again. Out
here I don't have to worry about disturbing

anyone else. And I guess I just needed some time on my own."

He didn't seem to want to say any more about it because he pointed with his chin toward the vegetables still piled in a colander and said, "Dry those for me, will you?"

"Sure," she agreed, setting down her glass of very mellow red wine and using a paper towel to do as he'd asked.

"Where did you learn to cook?" she asked then, attempting a new subject.

"Trial and error. During residency, Buzz— do you remember Buzz?"

"I do. From what I recall, the two of you were inseparable, closer even than you were with your own brother. And I know he was killed in action in Iraq. I was sorry to hear it."

Tate nodded but he didn't remark on her condolences. Instead he went on with what he'd been about to say.

"During residency, Buzz and I got an apartment across the street from the hospital—we were working insane hours, we were on call more than off, and never getting enough sleep. We decided that it might help if we didn't have to commute. But losing the commute also cost me having a chef to fix my meals and Buzz having his grandmother to cook for him. We got sick of frozen dinners and takeout, and that was when we both learned how to make a few quick and easy dishes to get us through."

Tanya had the impression that talking about his late friend raised a mixed bag of emotions in him so she didn't encourage him to say more.

She didn't have the burden of keeping the conversation going, though, because then Tate said, "What about you? Do you cook?"

"Some. As soon as I could, I moved out of the dorm at college. I couldn't afford takeout or anything fancy, but I got my fill of tuna and canned soup in a hurry and I had to figure something else out. Plus I put in some time working in the restaurant industry—I came away from that with a few tips."

"College was where?"

"Los Angeles. I went to the University of Southern California—your mother actually wrote one of my letters of recommendation and helped me get a scholarship."

"I didn't know," he admitted. "What's your degree in?"

"Broadcast journalism."

He took more vegetables to slice. "Putting

your energy into a degree like that is kind of risky, isn't it? What do you do with it if—"

"If someone does something underhanded and gets me taken off air?" she challenged.

He had the good grace to smile with some contrition. "Let's say, what if you grow a huge, unsightly, unremovable wart on the side of your nose and no news station on the planet will put your face on camera—what do you do with a broadcast journalism degree then?"

"There are jobs behind the camera that I could still do, but it's on-air time I'm after," she said, emphasizing each word to bring home her point.

He apparently decided to ignore her second jab because rather than respond to it, he said, "Why did you decide to come back here to work? Dallas is a big market for everything, but I'd think it would be flashier and more impressive to do the news in L.A. or New York or Washington."

"I interned in L.A. and worked there after I graduated. But the flashier, more impressive markets are also harder to break into and I didn't feel like I was on the fast track. Plus Mom never liked my living out of state or that far away from her, but she wouldn't move to where I was, so I finally decided to come back here. There's still the potential for climbing the ladder from a local independent station to a local network affiliate to one of the bigger markets, and maybe if that happens I'll be able to persuade her to come with me then. But the potential isn't there at all when... I'm...banned...from... even...the...local...independent...station," she said, speaking with even more exaggeration.

"I get the idea—I'm a low-down, dirty dog for sabotaging your big chance here. But let's not forget that what prompted *my* actions were *your* actions."

"All right, we'll call it a draw," she said as if she were being the bigger person.

It made him smile again as he finished with the vegetables and brought a plate of already-sliced beef from the refrigerator.

He tossed everything into the preheated wok where the sound of sizzling was loud enough to make it difficult to talk. Tanya didn't try and merely enjoyed the sight of Tate cooking.

He was as adept with that as he'd been with everything she'd seen him do at the clinic, and as she watched him it occurred to her that all the way around today she was getting a glimpse of him as not just someone born with a silver spoon in his mouth.

When he judged their meal ready he urged her to the small table nearby where two places were set. There was also a rice cooker and a plate that displayed three small bowls of what appeared to be sauces.

"Sweet, hot and spicy, not so hot," he described the sauces, aiming a long middle finger at each one and for some inexplicable reason, causing Tanya's focus to be on that finger rather than on the sauces. Or that finger and the thought of how even that was somehow sexy....

Then he retrieved the bottle of wine from where she'd left it after pouring her glass, and as they both sat down to eat Tanya determinedly reined in her mental wanderings.

"Did you wait tables or work in a fast-food place or a diner—or what—through college?" he asked after they'd tasted the food and Tanya had complimented his culinary skills.

She was a little surprised that he'd listened closely enough to what she'd said to recall her comment about having worked in the restaurant industry.

"We're supposed to be talking McCords and the jewelry business and the diamond, remember?" she reminded him before she got carried away thinking the fact that he was paying attention to what she said was anything special.

"The whole day was stuff you can use—the clinic is funded by my mother's charities and donations from McCord's Jewelers. I work there and oversee the rest of the staff to make sure the quality of care is the best that it can be. Now work is over for both of us," he decreed.

Tanya supposed she could concede to that. His small talk *was* staying within the bounds of propriety—it was only her own thoughts that had strayed. And while she would have liked to go on gathering material, she'd seen the day he'd put in and she had the sense that he needed a plain, ordinary, small talk–filled dinner, so she let him have it his way.

"Okay," she said, after another bite of the Asian-influenced cuisine. "Yes, I worked in a fast-food place—I was the bagel butterer on an assembly line at a sandwich shop. I also waited tables at one of those places that only serve breakfast—but I don't think you could call it a diner. And there was an upscale, fancy restaurant where I did some hostessing."

"So basically, you worked your way through college completely in the food industry."

"Basically, but not entirely. I also worked as a motel maid before I did any of that. But only for three days—"

"Three days?"

"That was all I could take. You can't imagine what kind of mess some people will leave in a motel room and the morning I found a dead guy was the day I quit—"

"You found a dead guy?" he asked, trying not to be amused.

"He'd died in his sleep, of a heart attack. But that was it for me—that was when I went with the restaurant work. Then, as soon as I could get on with a news station even just running errands, I grabbed it."

"I take it the scholarship wasn't all that great?" he said apologetically.

"No, it was," she assured him, not wanting to sound ungrateful. "I wasn't complaining. The scholarship paid my full tuition. But I had to earn money for books and fees and living expenses."

"I know you weren't complaining. I think

I was just feeling guilty because I partied and played my way through college."

"You partied and played your way through middle school and high school, too," she reminded him.

He smiled sheepishly. "That I did. In fact, I was thinking about you last night—about what I remembered of you growing up—"

"Not much, I'll bet," Tanya said, pushing away her plate because she'd eaten all she could.

His smile widened as he sat back, apparently finished eating as well. "Actually, I remembered that you were the you-shouldn't-do-that kid."

"You've lost me," she said, not sure what he was talking about.

"My most vivid memories of you are of looking up from something Buzz and I were about to do and seeing this big-eyed kid who had appeared out of nowhere to stand on the sidelines, very stoically shaking her head at me, and saying, *you shouldn't do that....*"

Tanya laughed. "I don't remember that."

"Oh, yeah. I remember because you were usually right. Of course I just thought you were some annoying little kid sticking her nose in where it didn't belong. But you were still right. The day Buzz and I tried out our dirt bikes on the front lawn—we were thirteen so you had to be—"

"Six."

"And you said, *you shouldn't do that, the gardener will get mad....*"

"And you did it anyway."

"And tore up the lawn. And the gardener *did* get mad, and so did my parents. I was grounded for two weeks. Then there was the time when we set up a ramp at the edge of the pool. We had new scooters and we were sure that with enough height we could jump the shallow end. There you were, doing your *you-shouldn't-do-that* thing again. I'm pretty sure I said something rude to you and told you to go away. You wouldn't go away and I figured I'd show you that you were nothing but a dumb kid. I ended up in the pool, destroyed the scooter and broke my leg. That cost me another two weeks of grounding."

Tanya laughed. "I honestly don't remember ever saying you shouldn't do anything."

"Then there was my party—"

"I remember the party. You were seventeen, I was ten. I watched from the bushes until my mom caught me. But I still don't recall a 'you shouldn't do that.'"

"Oh, yeah. I had permission to have twelve people over to swim that night. But nobody was going to be home so Buzz and I handed out flyers to everyone we knew and some people we didn't. We paid an older guy to buy beer and we were sneaking the kegs in the back and talking about what a huge, blowout bash the party was going to be. And again you appeared from out of nowhere to say—"

"You shouldn't do that?"

He pointed an index finger at her. "The you-shouldn't-do-that kid."

They both laughed.

"That one cost me a month out of my summer—I was going to get to stay home while my family vacationed in Italy but because of the party, my parents decided I couldn't be trusted and made me go with them."

Tanya shrugged. "Guess you shouldn't have done that," she joked as she stood and began to clear the table.

She half expected Tate to remain seated there while she did the work but he got up, too, and, side by side, they cleaned the dinner mess.

"What about you?" he asked as they did. "Did you go through your teens toeing the line like you thought I should have?"

"I kind of did, actually," she answered. "We might have grown up in the same general vicinity for the most part but, believe me, my life was completely different than yours. From the minute I was old enough to work I was expected to show responsibility by getting a job. So when I was here I worked in the ice cream shop—more food service. When I was with my grandparents I worked—"

"When you were with your grandparents? I didn't know you spent time away from here."

"Quite a bit of time. But that's a whole other story." And since the dishes were loaded into the dishwasher, his kitchen was in order again and it was getting late, she said, "A whole other story I'll save so we can call it a night—I promised my mother I'd be back before she went to bed and you must be tired yourself."

"Trouble sleeping, remember? But I

wouldn't want you to keep JoBeth up waiting for you."

And worrying that she was staying any later than was necessary...

Tate walked Tanya to the door and put his hand on the knob to open it for her. But rather than doing that, he stayed in that position while pausing to look at her with the door still closed.

"This was nice," he said as if that surprised him.

"It was. Thanks for dinner. You get points for today and points for your cooking talents, too."

"Points? I didn't know there was a scorecard."

"Not literally."

"And why did I get points for today?"

"Because what I saw of you was so eye-opening."

"In what way?"

"I don't remember the 'you shouldn't do thats.' But I do remember you doing some wild and reckless things in pursuit of fun and frolic—which was all I thought you were about. Mr. Good-Time. But today I saw for myself that there *is* more to you...."

Why had her voice gotten softer by the

end of that? Why had it sounded almost intimate? And why was she staring up at him and thinking that she really was seeing him through new eyes? And that she liked what she was seeing so much more than when she'd thought he was just a handsome face....

"Anyway," she said, trying for a more normal tone and to halt the thoughts and feelings that were suddenly running through her. "I admired what I saw of what you did today and it will definitely be a part of the collage of the McCords."

He smiled. "I was impressed with you today, too," he said. "I wasn't sure if you were all talk or not, but you dug right in. And you didn't even flinch when old Nesbit came wandering out of recovery in the buff."

Tanya laughed. "*That* I won't be reporting on," she said. "Though you were really quick with that chart you held in front of his dangling participles so the lady I was giving juice to didn't see much."

"Dangling participles? Things were definitely dangling...." he said wryly, laughing too.

Tanya was having a much better time than she wished she was. It made it hard for her to make herself leave. And Tate wasn't encouraging it—he was still standing there with the door closed, looking down at her.

And it wasn't just *any* look in those clear blue eyes. He was looking at her in a way other men had looked at her. Just before they'd kissed her...

Was he thinking about it? Tanya wondered.

Because she was...

You shouldn't do that—the phrase that had been repeated so much tonight echoed through her head. And she knew it was true, that kissing him wasn't what she should do. Or let him do.

Even if something in her was shouting for him to go ahead and do it....

Then he cocked his head just a bit to one side. But Tanya couldn't tell if he was even aware that he'd done it because he was staring so intently, so deeply into her eyes.

He leaned forward. Barely. Almost not at all.

Her chin went up about the same amount, on its own.

Shouldn't do that...

Except that she wanted to.

She really, really wanted to....

But maybe the mere thought that they shouldn't do that somehow transmitted to Tate, who finally took heed of it. He straightened up again and turned the handle to open the door so she could go out.

Which was exactly what she knew she had to do. She had to get out of there before she did something stupid....

"Tomorrow?" she said as she stepped across the threshold, stopping only when she felt the cooler night air on her face to turn and look at him from a greater distance than had separated them in the house.

"I have surgeries scheduled all day and dinner with the family tomorrow evening. But I've left orders for all the family albums to be dragged out of storage—I thought maybe we could go through them tomorrow night after dinner. That should give you a fairly decent family history."

Why did tomorrow night seem so far away? And why was she thinking about how endlessly the hours would drag on instead of being aggravated by the fact that the entire next day would be wasted?

But that was how it was and she couldn't help it. She could only hope the time would pass quickly....

"Okay," she heard herself say compliantly. "If that's how it has to be."

"Unfortunately..." he said so quietly that she had the feeling he regretted having to wait, too.

But that couldn't be, Tanya told herself. *He's engaged—don't forget that....*

She said good-night then and headed in the direction of her mother's bungalow. But since she hadn't heard the guesthouse door close, just before she stepped onto the path that led through trees and bushes and would take her out of sight, she glanced over her shoulder.

There was Tate, standing in the doorway watching her.

And thinking what? About kissing her?

Had he almost kissed her or had she been wrong about that?

She must have been wrong.

But right or wrong, there would be no kissing of Tate McCord! she told herself.

Still, she thought he *had* almost kissed her.

And even though she knew it would have been a mistake, even though she knew it couldn't happen, as she slipped out of his sight down the path to the bungalow, she

was wishing that this might have been one
of those times—like all those others—when
he'd ignored the you-shouldn't-do-that and
done it anyway....

Chapter Five

"Katie. Hi," Tate said into his cell phone when it rang on his way to work Tuesday morning and the display let him know in advance who his caller was.

"I hope I didn't wake you," Katie replied to his greeting.

"No, I'm about five minutes away from the hospital. How's everything?"

"Okay. As well as could be expected, I suppose," Katie said.

Tate had known her long enough to think he knew all of her moods, but he couldn't pinpoint this one. Trying to, he said, "You sound tired."

"I didn't have the chance to tell my parents that the engagement is off until last night. You know how it is—there have been dinners and parties and people around since I got to Key West and I had to wait for a moment alone with them."

"And I don't imagine that they welcomed the news," Tate guessed, not eager to tell his own family for just that reason.

"No, they certainly didn't *welcome* it. They were actually very impatient with me."

"I'm sorry," Tate said sympathetically.

"It was no worse than I thought it would be, but still…" Katie sighed. "After all this time they were sure their dreams were finally coming true. I knew they weren't going to be happy to have me wake them up."

"What about you?" Tate asked point-blank because he still wasn't getting a clear read on Katie's feelings. And while he knew breaking up was for the best, he was concerned about her.

"Well, I *am* tired—you were right about that. We were up arguing until very late and I had an early hair appointment this morning so I couldn't sleep in. But otherwise…"

There was a pause that didn't convince Tate that Katie was merely worn out.

Then she continued. "I'm a little at loose ends. You *were* always sort of my guy," she said with a laugh that helped him believe she wasn't doing too badly despite the fact that she might be a little down in the dumps over the way things had turned out.

"Even when we weren't together," she went on, "there was always just that thought that we'd probably end up with each other some day. And it isn't as if I don't care about you, Tate—"

"Same here."

"But I truly do think there's more out there for both of us."

Why did Tanya pop into his mind at that exact moment?

But Katie was still talking and he forced himself to pay attention.

"—it just isn't easy to start over. I keep thinking that I haven't ever been in a single, long-term, committed relationship with any-one of my own choosing. That was part of the argument last night—I said I needed to be able to decide who the man for me would be. But just between us, the whole time I was wondering if I'll know *how* to choose someone for myself."

Tate laughed. "I'm pretty sure you just go

with whoever you have the strongest feelings for," he said. And again—for no reason that made sense—Tanya came to mind.

"What about you?" Katie asked then. "How are you?"

"I'm doing all right," he said.

"You sound better than *all right*. You sound a little more like your old self. Were you that glad to get rid of me?"

"Come on, you know better than that," he chastised. "And I didn't *get rid* of you. If anybody got rid of anybody—"

"I'm saying it was a mutual decision. And now you can, too—that's why I wanted to talk to you first thing this morning. My mother is threatening to call yours. I asked her to wait but I don't know how long she will. So don't put off telling Eleanor or it'll be my mother who does."

"I'm having dinner with the family tonight. I'll tell them then."

"I hope it goes smoother with yours than it did with mine."

"Even if it doesn't, it'll all blow over before long," Tate assured her as he pulled into the doctors' parking lot of Meridian General.

"It's nice that we can still chat like this, though," Katie said then. "And be friends…"

"That isn't going to change—we've always been friends, we always will be friends. You know if there's anything you need from me you just have to ask, right?"

"Same here," she echoed his earlier words. "I should let you go, though, I just heard the parking lot attendant say good morning to you so you must be at the hospital. I'll try to keep my mother from calling yours at least until tomorrow."

"Thanks."

"And I'll see you at the Labor Day party—I should probably apologize to you ahead of time for anything my parents might say to you at that."

The McCords were throwing one of their lavish soirees to mark the end of the summer season and Katie's family was always at the top of the guest list.

"Don't worry about it. It'll be fine," Tate assured her once more.

"I hope so," Katie said. "I hope everything will be fine for us both."

"It will be."

"Well, one way or another, I just wanted you to know that you're free to tell whoever you want now. And thanks for letting me go first with the families."

"Sure."

They said their goodbyes then and Tate turned off his phone as he parked in his assigned spot.

But the freedom he now had to get the word out that he was no longer engaged to Katie was still on his mind.

Of course it was his family who had to be next to know.

But right after that?

For the third time it was Tanya who made an instant appearance in his head.

Because Tanya was really the only person he *wanted* to tell....

"The engagement is off? Oh, Tate..."

Tate had waited until everyone was finishing dessert Tuesday evening to make his announcement. Not that *everyone* was there. His mother, Eleanor, was at the head of the table and her response to the news was rife with disappointment and disapproval. His older brother Blake was sitting across from him, and one of his younger twin sisters, Penny, was to his right. But even without the rest of the family there, Tate knew word would spread to Penny's twin, Paige, and to his youngest brother, Charlie, and he hadn't wanted to delay telling his mother until Paige and Charlie were around, as well.

"These breakups are never for good," Blake said with an annoyed sigh.

"It's time the *breakups* stop," Eleanor said. "I know you've been in a bad way since we lost Buzz, Tate. But I honestly think the path out of it is to finally do what you should have done long ago—stop this seesaw you and Katie have always been on and take a definitive step into your future with the woman you know you're going to end up with eventually."

"In other words, little brother," Blake said, "it's time for you to grow up."

Tate could have taken issue with that but he didn't. "What it is time for," he said instead, "is for Katie and me to get off the seesaw once and for all."

"What can you possibly be thinking?" Blake demanded, surprising Tate with a reaction that was stronger than Tate had expected from his brother. Blake should have had enough on his mind with the current business problems and trying to find the Santa Magdalena diamond to make this low on his list of concerns. "Why don't you open your eyes and take a look at what you have in Katie?" Blake continued. "You keep going back to her—you must recognize on some level how terrific she is. What will it take for you to just accept that you aren't going to do better?"

"You don't know what you're talking about, Blake," Tate said calmly. "I do know how terrific Katie is. But when there isn't that…certain something…between two people, you can be terrific, she can be terrific, it just doesn't make any difference. And I'm sure you think this was my idea, but the truth is, it came about at her instigation."

"Isn't that exactly what I told you the other night?" Blake said with disgust. "You took her for granted, you neglected her and now she's called things off."

"Ultimately, it was a mutual decision," Tate said, borrowing from Katie. "At her instigation, but a mutual decision. We both agreed that all these years have been more about what the families wanted, what the families pressured us into, and not about our feelings for each other. But the bottom line—" Tate said, thinking that his brother was a bottom-line kind of person "—is that we don't have the kind of feelings that end in marriage. At least not a happy, lasting marriage. And since—for some reason— you seem to have adopted the role of Katie's champion, isn't that what you'd want for her? To be married to someone she's actually in love with and has a chance to be happy with for the rest of her life?"

"It goes without saying that that's what I'd want for her. For you both," Blake added impatiently.

"Well, we've come to the conclusion that that isn't what we'd have together."

"That's the conclusion you've come to this week. Or this month," Eleanor said as if she was at her wits' end with him. "But next week or next month, you'll be telling us you're back together again. Just stop this on and off!"

"We have stopped it, only we've stopped it at *off*," Tate said, concealing how much he wanted this to end because he was itching to get to Tanya to go through the family albums the way they'd planned. "This is it for Katie and me, whether the families like it or not," he concluded firmly.

"And *families* shouldn't enter into a person's relationships," Penny said then, chiming in for the first time.

Tate appreciated his younger sister's support but it surprised him, too. Penny was the quieter, more introverted of the twins. She didn't often venture into a family fray unless she had to.

"Talk to us when you have a *relationship* that the family enters into, Penny," Blake said sardonically.

"That's what I'm worried about—the family entering into *my* relationship," Penny muttered under her breath and with some defensiveness that seemed out of place.

"What does *that* mean?" Blake asked with a chuckle, as if Penny were six years old rather than twenty-six.

Tate saw how much that irked Penny— she sat up straighter, her lips pursed. Then she said, "I've…"

She stopped herself as if to gauge her words.

"It's okay, Penny," Tate said. "I appreciate that you're on my side, but you don't have to fight my battles."

"It isn't only your battle," his sister answered as if she'd just that moment come to some kind of decision.

Then she made an announcement of her own. "I've been seeing Jason Foley."

That came as far, far more of a shock

than Tate's broken engagement and brought several moments of stunned silence before Blake broke it.

"Jason Foley?" he repeated in disbelief.

"What do you mean you're seeing him? As a friend?" Eleanor asked in a controlled tone.

"More than friends," Penny said.

"You're *dating?*" their mother pressed, beginning to sound alarmed.

Penny hesitated. She was a private person and Tate realized this wasn't easy for her.

But then she said, "Yes, we're dating."

"That's bad, Penny," Blake decreed. "You know the Foleys hate us, that they've been convinced for decades that we cheated them out of the land, and now with the potential that the diamond could be—"

"This doesn't have anything to do with that," Penny insisted.

"Don't kid yourself!" Blake said in a louder voice. "Don't you think it's just a little suspicious that now—of *all* times—there's a Foley sniffing around? They're looking for a way in, Penny! For information about the diamond!"

"You haven't actually given me any information about the diamond except to en-

list me to design jewelry that will tie into it
if you find it."

"I don't want the Foleys knowing even
that much. That's what they're after—any
crumb they can get their hands on and use!"
Blake shouted.

Tate was aware of how invested Blake
was in the business, in finding the diamond,
in using it to salvage McCord's Jewelers.
He knew his brother was under pressure he
wasn't willing to share unless it was absolutely necessary because Blake always believed he was the best person to shoulder the
load. And Tate thought that because of all
that, it didn't occur to Blake how insulting
to Penny it was to imply that Jason Foley
was interested in her only as some kind of
ploy. Even though Tate agreed that it was a
possibility.

"We don't know that that's why Jason
Foley is seeing Penny, Blake," he said.

"I know nothing good can come of a Mc-
Cord getting involved with a Foley."

"Charlie came of it," Penny said, using the
information their mother had only recently
shared with them that the youngest McCord
was the result of an affair Eleanor had had
with Rex Foley twenty-two years earlier.

But it was information that had caused all of Eleanor's children to give her a wide berth ever since. To Tate's knowledge, none of them had discussed it with their mother in any depth, even since Eleanor's return that morning to take care of the last details of the Labor Day party. So Tate could hardly believe his ears when Penny used that information for her own purposes now.

Glancing at his mother, Tate found her unruffled by it, though. Instead, venturing delicately into the subject that still wasn't easy for any of them to accept, Eleanor said, "Yes, Penny, Charlie *did* come of my involvement with a Foley. But that's why I can speak from experience and tell you that a tie between a Foley and a McCord is a rocky road."

"We just don't want you to get hurt, Penny," Tate added.

"That's true," Eleanor confirmed.

"What's *true,*" Penny countered, "is that whatever is between two *families* shouldn't interfere with what might—or might not— be between two individual people. Not when it comes to you and Katie, Tate, and not when it comes to whoever I'm with, either. Jason and I are seeing each other and it doesn't have anything to do with the fact that I'm a McCord and he's a Foley. It doesn't have anything to do with an old feud, or with land that changed hands a gazillion years ago, or with a diamond. It's *in spite* of all that and it's only about Jason and me."

"I hope you're right," Eleanor said with worry lines creasing her brow.

"I'm telling you," Blake seemed unable to keep from reiterating, "you don't know what the Foleys could be up to."

"It may be perfectly innocent," Tate contributed. "Jason Foley may just be carried away by how terrific *you* are. But be careful—that's all we're asking. When it comes to a Foley, be really careful…."

Chapter Six

Tate was sitting at one of the poolside tables when Tanya came out from the wooded path after leaving her mother's cottage Tuesday night. The moment she stepped through the clearing in the bushes and magnolia trees she saw that he was watching for her and a small smile turned up the corners of his mouth.

Why *that* sent something gooshy through her, she didn't know, but that bare hint of him being pleased to see her was all it took to heat her from the inside out.

Then his gaze went from her free-falling hair, down the teal T-shirt she was wearing to her flowing wide-leg slacks as she crossed to him. His smile grew bigger. And that internal heat took on a rosy, sensual glow.

Stop it! she ordered herself, trying to keep uppermost in her mind that in spite of the fact that it was late evening, that they were suddenly together again, under a clear moonlit sky, this was about work. *Only* work...

"Finally!" Tate muttered when she reached him, before she'd even said hello.

"You just called me five minutes ago to tell me to come over," she said, thinking he was making a comment about having to wait for her.

He shook his head. *"Finally* we can get to what we had planned tonight."

"Ah," Tanya said as she took the chair nearest him.

What they had planned tonight was to look through his family albums. And since there was a stack of them on the table, she sat where they would each be able to see them. It didn't have anything to do with the fact that she *wanted* to sit close to him. Want to or not, she swore that she wasn't going to let this evolve into anything more than doing her job tonight.

"I brought the wine I started on at dinner. Will you have some?" Tate asked then, picking up the open bottle and refreshing his own glass while he indicated the clean glass beside it.

"This is supposed to be work for me," Tanya reminded them both, holding up her notepad and pen to prove it.

"Sometimes mixing business and pleasure is a good thing," he enticed.

"I hope that isn't your philosophy when you do surgery," she countered.

That merely made him laugh and question her again by holding the bottle higher.

She shouldn't. This *was* work.

And yet she heard herself say "Maybe just one glass."

She set her pad and pen on the table as he poured, using his averted glance as an opportunity to give him the once-over. The pool area where they were sitting was well lit and she could tell that he'd dressed for dinner and then undone some of it for this. There wasn't a suitcoat or tie anywhere around, but he had on gray slacks and a crisp white shirt with the long sleeves rolled to his elbows. He was also clean shaven, the scent of his cologne just barely wafted to her and his slightly longish hair was neatly combed.

Would it have helped if he'd looked grungy? she asked herself, knowing her vow to keep this out of the realm of another datelike evening with him was already weakening.

But somehow she doubted that the way he was dressed made any difference. The man just seemed to hold an appeal for her that she didn't fully understand. Maybe he'd unearthed some kind of deep-seated attraction to unavailable men that she hadn't known she possessed.

But he *was* unavailable—in so many ways—and she told herself not to forget that.

When the wine was poured and the bottle replaced on the table, Tate handed her her glass and lounged back in his chair with a deep sigh of what sounded like relief.

"Rough day?" Tanya asked as she took a sip of the wine.

"Rough dinner," he amended.

There was talk among the staff about the tense state the family had been in since rumors had begun to surface that Tate's mother had announced that her youngest son, Charlie, was a Foley. None of the staff knew any of the details, but they did know that Charlie had almost instantly gone off to settle back into college early, and that Eleanor had taken some time away herself.

Tanya assumed that tensions over Charlie's paternity were still the cause of the rough dinner, but Tate didn't offer her any explanation as she took another sip of wine.

"So, how far back would you like to go?" Tate asked with a nod toward the albums.

Good, he is getting right down to business, Tanya told herself to ward off a ridiculous sense of disappointment that he wasn't bothering with small talk tonight.

"I did some background research today and thought about how I'd like to do this," she said, trying to sound purely professional. "I'd like a clear picture of the McCords and your family history first. Once that's accomplished, I can get into the story of the diamond and the treasure and of the feud with the Foleys, and the land and silver mines that changed hands, too. But for tonight, how about starting with just the family stuff?"

"Whatever you want."

"And since it looks as though the feud between the Foleys and the McCords began with Gavin Foley and Harry McCord—"

"My grandfather."

"—that seems like the furthest we need to go in McCord family history."

"Okay, Harry McCord it is," Tate said, sitting up and reaching for the albums. He discarded two of the more ragged ones before settling on one that displayed old, poor-quality black-and-white photographs of a man who bore a clear resemblance to him. "These are of my grandfather in front of the silver mines that launched the McCord fortune and, ultimately, McCord's Jewelers," he informed her.

Tanya flipped through page after page, noting that there were five mines, all of them with a large stone at their entrance, each with a petroglyph carved into it to name it. The Turtle mine. The Eagle mine. The Lizard. The Tree. The Bow.

"Can I have a few of these pictures to use? I'll make sure they're returned," Tanya said when she'd reached the end of that album.

"I don't see why not," Tate agreed, taking them out and giving them to her.

"So, was your father Harry McCord's only child?" Tanya asked then.

"No. My father was the oldest son. The

younger—my Uncle Joseph—lives in Italy. You must know Gabby? My cousin?"

Gabriella McCord was a famous model and it was nearly impossible to pick up any magazine, newspaper or tabloid and not find her face on the cover. So Tanya felt a little stupid for not having considered from where on the family tree Gabby McCord had sprouted. She didn't admit it, though.

"I know *of* her," Tanya said. "The whole world knows *of* her. But it isn't as if she was ever introduced to the housekeeper's daughter on one of her visits, and I had no idea how she fit into the family—I guess I'd never really thought about it."

"Well, Gabby's father is Joseph. Joseph married an Italian actress descended from royalty over there. They made their home in Italy, and Joseph oversees and manages the European branches of McCord's Jewelers. My grandmother died in childbirth with Joseph." Tate found a picture of his grandmother and a few of Joseph growing up and as an adult, showing them to Tanya.

"So Harry McCord raised Devon—your father—and your uncle on his own?"

"That's the story. My father said one of his earliest memories was of going out to the mines with my grandfather, and that was where he and Joseph spent most of their time growing up—if they weren't in school, they were working alongside my grandfather."

Tate moved on to the next album, flipping through more shots of the brothers Devon and Joseph until he reached one of them with Harry McCord, standing outside of McCord's Jewelers.

"That was the first store," Tate said.

Tanya took a close look at the nondescript glass storefront that could hardly compare to the current McCord's Jewelers. Now they were known for their marble entrances, their plush lavender and gray carpeting, their mirrored cases and velvet displays, their leather club chairs for shopping in comfort. And their new customer-pampering campaign had only increased the level of luxury that was a world of difference from that initial jewelry shop.

"You've come a long way," she observed.

"That was my father's doing. And Blake's. I take no credit for what goes on with the jewelry business."

"I'd like to use this picture of the original store."

"Go ahead."

Tanya took it to put with the others she was collecting.

Then they moved on to the next album. It contained pictures of Devon McCord's wedding to Tate's mother, the beautiful, blonde Eleanor Holden.

"Huh," Tanya said as she glanced through them.

"What?"

"Your mother is the most somber-looking bride I think I've ever seen, and your father looks more victorious than smitten."

"That seems about right," Tate said, leaning in for a closer look and giving Tanya a better whiff of his cologne that was more heady than the wine she was slowly sipping.

"Why does that seem about right?" she asked.

"That my father looked victorious? That was always how he was when it came to my mother."

Devon McCord had only died a year ago but while Tanya remembered the man, she had never paid any attention to his relationship with his wife, so this was news to her.

"What do you mean?" she said.

"Some of it goes back to the problems

with the Foleys—my mother dated both my father and Rex Foley, you know?"

"No, I didn't know that," Tanya said, her interest sparked.

"I don't really know much about it except that she did. The only thing I know is that my father would say—*Rex Foley wanted her but I got her.* Only he didn't say it as if it made him a lucky man—which was how I always thought he *should* have said it. He'd say it as if she were the spoils of war. Just one more thing he'd won out over the Foleys, as if it wasn't my mother who mattered as much as his victory over Rex Foley."

"And now your dad is gone and you find out that Rex Foley is Charlie's father...."

Tanya knew her mother would be furious with her if JoBeth found out she was taking such a liberty with a McCord. The McCords probably didn't even realize that the staff was aware of what was going on within the family, and certainly no employee—or employee's daughter—was at liberty to inquire about it.

But at that moment Tanya wasn't there as the housekeeper's daughter. She was there as an investigative reporter. And that meant asking even the probing, off-limits questions.

Tate didn't answer it readily. He sat back, he took a drink of his wine, he raised a single eyebrow at her. "Hard to keep a secret from the staff," he said.

Tanya raised both of her eyebrows back at him, committing blame to no one.

"It's a private matter," he said then in a tone that warned her not to pursue the subject. "We're all still trying to come to grips with it. We definitely don't want it announced in a news report. But then, that seems to fall more into the category of gossip than what you said you want to do."

Tanya had to smile at his attempt to manipulate her. "I don't know—two of Dallas's preeminent families who have been in a long-standing feud, now connected by blood because the head of one of the families had an affair with the head of the other? That makes for a thin line between gossip and news. Especially in a piece like this."

"Affair?" Tate repeated as if she were overstating.

"It *wasn't* an affair?"

Tate's sky-blue eyes bored into her for a moment as if he were sizing her up. Or judging just how much of a problem she could be for him. Gone was the openness she'd seen more of recently, replaced by a cool aloofness and the much harder edge she'd seen in him on Friday night in the library.

Then he sighed again and said, "I'm going to be straight with you—I don't really know what went on between my mother and Rex Foley. I know—have always known—that she *dated* Rex Foley when they were teenagers. I don't think there was anything between them once she married my father, and how they got together again is a mystery to me. I know—hell, you might even remember—that my parents' marriage hit a rough patch and they separated. Charlie was conceived during that separation so obviously my mother turned to Rex Foley then, but I have no idea how that came about. Has she been involved with Rex Foley since then? I don't know and to tell you the truth, I don't want to know. Whatever happened is my mother's business."

There was no question in Tanya's mind that she'd just poured salt into an open wound. And what that had done was reawaken the new—and not necessarily improved—Tate, just when she'd been getting a little more of the old.

Tanya had to admit that the new Tate was

far more daunting. But it was her job to be undaunted.

"How is the fact that your mother had—or has—a relationship with Rex Foley affecting your family?"

"Right now, I'd say that we're all just a little dumbfounded. Who knows what will happen in the future?"

"Have feelings changed toward Charlie?"

"No. Charlie is what he's always been—our brother."

"Now he's also brother to the Foleys...."

Tate didn't like this direction. He frowned at her. "We all have our flaws," he said in a clipped voice she'd never heard him use before.

"Being half Foley is a flaw?" she ventured anyway.

"Are you going to make me sorry I agreed to do this?" Tate demanded suddenly.

"Probably."

There was a moment of silence during which Tate gave her the hardest stare she'd ever had. Tanya actually thought he might get up, walk away and let her suffer the consequences of snooping through the library on Friday night. She thought it was a very real possibility that he might just have her fired from the studio, fire her mother as housekeeper and generally wreak havoc on her life rather than continue this.

But then his handsome face eased into an unexpected smile again and he shook his head. "I don't know if being half Foley is a flaw or not," he finally answered. "Right now it's confusing for us all—especially for Charlie—and I think we just have to wait and see how it plays out."

He said that with enough finality to let her know he wasn't going to say any more on this topic.

So Tanya switched gears.

"I suppose McCord's Jewelers' financial woes are more of a priority than Charlie's parentage at this point, anyway," she said.

"Strike two! You really are aiming to tick me off tonight, aren't you?" Tate said, though with a hint of humor infusing his words.

"Just doing my job. There *are* rumors that the family business is floundering and from what I overheard Friday night, the rumors have some foundation in truth—that makes it part of the story," she insisted.

"The jewelry business is Blake's bailiwick and the only thing I'll say, the only thing I know to report, is that he's working to increase sales the way any number of businesses do—with new advertising or new packaging or new whatever. That doesn't mean anything is *floundering.*"

"I've seen the ads—A Once In A Lifetime Experience," Tanya said. "Coffee and pastries for morning shoppers. Champagne and hors d'oeuvres later in the day. One-on-one customer service—"

"And Gabby—don't forget Gabby is available by email for personal shopping advice for certain clients who want to know what a high-profile trendsetter would buy."

"That sounds like you're putting in a plug for Blake's new public relations campaign."

Tate merely smiled as if that was exactly what he was doing and was pleased to be able to again control the information that would go into her story.

But she couldn't let him get too comfortable. "And I heard you and Blake talk about him stockpiling canary diamonds to use as a tie-in with the Santa Magdalena diamond *when* he finds it."

Tate sobered and sighed again. "You're just digging around all over the place, aren't you?"

Tanya gave him the that's-my-job shrug.

"Let's just say," Tate said, "that it wouldn't do any harm to have the Santa Magdalena diamond appear. And I *hope* that that happens and the focus of your report leans more in that direction—in a direction that can *help* rather than hurt."

"In other words, you'd like it if my report could be more in the way of free advertisement than anything really revealing."

He just grinned.

"So you're using me? Is that why your fiancée isn't putting the kibosh on your spending so much time with me?"

"My *fiancée*..." He took a drink of his wine, looked at the glass as he set it back on the table then said, "No more fiancée. No more engagement."

"Oh..." she said, not impressed by the announcement.

He cocked his head at her. "You don't believe me?"

"Oh, sure," she said flimsily.

"You *don't* believe me."

"Believe you, don't believe you—it isn't really a matter of that. If the engagement was on yesterday and off today, it'll just be on again tomorrow."

"Even the staff—and the staff's family—has been keeping track of that?"

"Hard not to. One day you're an item, the next you aren't."

He shook his head. "Well, I hate to switch things up, but it's not the same this time. The engagement is definitely off."

Something about the way he said that gave Tanya a strange moment of elation that she tempered in a hurry. Then she shook her head at him, denying her own response and his claim all at once.

"You *still* don't believe me?" Tate interpreted that part of the head shake.

"It doesn't matter. This is how things go with you two. It stands to reason that you wouldn't make it to the altar the first time around. There will probably be a couple of engagements and breakups before that will happen. But do I think it will *eventually* happen? Sure."

Tate rolled his eyes. "This is tonight's dinner all over again."

So the subject that had made his family meal rough hadn't been the Charlie issue, it had been Tate's broken engagement....

"Your family didn't take it seriously either?" Tanya asked.

"Only seriously enough to be annoyed. But I *am* serious—Katie and I are—"

"I know, broken up."

"Once and for all."

Why was there that part of her that wanted so much to buy the finality he was selling? To think that it was even a possibility that Tate McCord and Katie Whitcomb-Salgar could be no more for real? It shouldn't have any impact on her at all, one way or another.

And yet it did. It raised a hope in her that was completely out of place. That shouldn't have been there. That she didn't *want* there. It made her feel as if she were walking a tightrope and had just discovered she didn't have a safety net. It shook her.

And she suddenly felt the need to get out of there. To get some distance in which to gather her wits and regain some balance. Some distance that would take her where Tate wasn't right there beside her, smelling so good, looking so good, and now not engaged....

"I think we've done enough here tonight," she said, getting to her feet. "We've laid the groundwork. We can probably call it quits."

She knew that had come out of the blue and the hastiness of it had obviously confused Tate. "We haven't even talked about the present-day McCords—with the exception of Gabby," he pointed out.

"I know about the present-day Mc-Cords," Tanya said as she closed her notebook, clipped her pen to it and began to make a pile of the photographs she was taking. "Your mother looks after the household and family and does charity work. Blake is the CEO of McCord's Jewelers. You're a surgeon. There's the twins, Penny and Paige—Penny is a jewelry designer, Paige is a geologist and gemologist. And there's Charlie, who's a student at Southern Methodist University and who we've also talked about tonight. Did I leave anyone out?"

"No, that's the lot of us," Tate confirmed, his tone still perplexed.

He stood then, too. And while Tanya hoped it was just a polite acknowledgment that she was about to leave, instead he said, "I'll walk you back to your mother's place."

"That's okay, you don't have to," she said, wishing it hadn't sounded so panicky.

"I want to," he assured her.

"Whatever," Tanya said, trying for aloofness and failing as she picked up everything and held it in front of her like a schoolgirl carrying books. Carrying books close and tight and protectively.

"Did I tick *you* off somehow?" Tate asked as they headed for the path that wound away from the pool.

"No. I don't know why you would think that."

"Maybe because you're acting as if I just grew fangs or something. Is my *not* being engaged scary to you?"

Terrifying. Although she wasn't exactly sure why, except possibly that she was terrified that she might give in to that wave of elation that had washed through her when he'd told her his engagement was off and let down her guard with him.

But if she let down her guard, then what? She could end up just another person he occupied his time with while he was on one of his innumerable breaks from Katie Whitcomb-Salgar. And all Tanya could think was, *Oh, no, not me.*

She just wasn't sure she could stick to it.

Although there *was* still the issue of her mother and her mother's job, and the fact that Tate was her mother's employer....

Reminding herself of that helped. It actually allowed her to begin to relax again.

Even if Tate wasn't engaged any longer, there was still a good—a *very* good—reason why she absolutely couldn't and wouldn't let anything happen with him. Anything even like last night when she'd thought he might be on the verge of kissing her.

Then something else that seemed completely unlikely occurred to her and compelled her to say, "When did this particular breakup come about? I didn't think Katie was even in Dallas."

"We broke up about a week ago but she wanted to tell her parents before word got out and I agreed to that. She is in Florida with them. She called this morning to let me know our private gag order was lifted and I could tell whoever I wanted."

So the engagement had been axed before Tate had found Tanya in the library on Friday night. It didn't have anything to do with the fact that he might be entertaining some notion of diddling the help's daughter.

Tanya was relieved that that hadn't been the case. That she hadn't had anything to do with this particular breakup. She was also glad that she hadn't said anything along those lines that would have embarrassed her. She was a little embarrassed anyway that she'd even had such a thought. Which was probably—like her thoughts of him kissing her—nothing but some kind of flight of fancy that she wasn't even sure why she was having.

And she should just stop it, she told herself. Stop the flights of fancy, stop thinking anything was going on between them. And while she was at it, stop thinking about him every minute of the day and night, the way she had been!

They'd reached her front door when Tate said, "We haven't talked about tomorrow."

"No, we haven't," Tanya answered glibly, slowly settling down and coming to grips with herself and his news.

"I have to make my rounds in the morning, but I'm free in the afternoon. I thought I'd give you a tour of the McCord contributions to the city and end with an evening under the stars."

Tanya glanced up to the sky and then dropped her gaze to blue eyes that were watching her intently. "Isn't that what we just had? An evening under the stars?"

"I have something a *little* bit different in mind. What do you say?"

"Is it all for my report?" she asked to

make it clear that that was the only thing she would agree to.

"Every bit of it," he assured without hesitation.

"Then okay."

"You still haven't answered my question about if my being *un*-engaged is somehow scary, though," he said then, smiling slightly.

"No, you're being un-engaged is not scary," she said as if the question itself was silly.

"You honestly did just decide on the spur of the moment that it was time to stop working tonight?"

"Yes. Why would I care if you're engaged or not?"

Okay, she'd been doing so well and then she'd gone and taken it too far by sounding defensive.

"I care," he said quietly, pointedly, continuing to gaze into her eyes.

And then she felt rotten. If he had been anyone else and this had been any other situation, she wouldn't have reacted the way she had to the revelation that he and the woman he'd intended to marry had ended things. She would have been more caring, more compassionate. She wouldn't have thought about herself.

"I'm sorry," she apologized. "I guess I was kind of callous. Even if you have had a lot of ups and downs in your relationship, that doesn't mean that you wouldn't be upset—"

"I'm not upset," he said. "And I don't mean to sound callous either, and maybe sometime I'll tell you why this *didn't* upset me, but what I do care about is that now I don't have to pretend that I'm committed to something—or someone—I'm not committed to."

"Because you're a bad secret-keeper?"

"Because I wanted to do this and I couldn't," he said, surprising her by coming in for the briefest, lightest, faintest of kisses.

A kiss Tanya didn't even have time to close her eyes for or respond to. And yet, a kiss that still managed to leave her lips tingling and her pulse racing.

But in spite of that, when it was over she shook her head at him. "Engaged or not, you can't do that," she said firmly.

"Why not?" he asked, smiling as if it was him who wasn't taking her seriously now.

"My mother works for you."

"I know that doesn't make for the most ideal situation, but—"

"But nothing," Tanya managed to sound so much stronger in her convictions than she felt. Especially since she was willing him with every ounce of her being to kiss her again...

Tate's smile went crooked—and almost too sexy and endearing to resist—before he said, "I do love a challenge."

"I'm not a challenge, I'm the housekeeper's daughter."

He nodded but she wasn't convinced that their very different social positions meant as much to him as it needed to.

Then, rather than address it again, he merely said, "I'll call you when I finish with rounds tomorrow. Plan on all afternoon and evening."

"To compile data for my report and that's it?" she said with a warning note in her voice.

"Nose to the grindstone all the way," he assured her.

"Okay," Tanya agreed a second time.

"See you then," he said.

Tanya nodded and watched him go, trying not to drink in every detail of his backside, of the confident swagger to his walk. Trying not to wish he was still standing in front of her instead, kissing her again. Kissing her more thoroughly than he had. His arms around her. Hers around him. Her hands slipping down to that very, very fine derriere she watched disappear into the shadows of the trees.

He's not engaged anymore....

The thought ran through her head like a wood nymph, taunting her. Tantalizing her.

But she chased it away.

Engaged, not engaged, it was all the same to her. She had more reasons than that not to give in to the attraction that kept sneaking in and taking over.

But it *did* keep sneaking in.

And taking over.

And the only way she had to combat it at that moment was to also remind herself that the odds of his not-engaged status lasting were slim to none.

And there was no way she was going to let herself be his hiatus-honey.

Chapter Seven

Tate was still thinking about Tuesday night—and Tanya—on Wednesday as he drove home from making rounds at the hospital.

Not that it was unusual these days for him to be thinking about Tanya. But what had her on his mind today was trying to figure out what had happened last night. One minute they'd been talking and—he'd thought—having a good time, and the next minute the tone had changed and she was up and out of there. In a hurry.

It had been obvious that it was the news about his broken engagement that had put a damper on things. But why? Why should that have caused her to shy away?

Certainly there was nothing about it that *should* have sent her running into the night. Or reacting like his family, either.

He had no idea what would put Tanya's response in the same category as his mother's and Blake's, but even if it was just in the same general ballpark—even if Tanya had felt some kind of affront to all of womankind—he hated the thought that something about him or something that he'd done had put her off like that.

It didn't bother him that his family might be disgusted that he was once again not following through with Katie. But Tanya? That was something else entirely. It bothered him that Tanya might think badly of him.

It bothered the hell out of him....

And that was new.

Caring what someone thought of him? He'd gone through his life not really considering what anyone thought about him. Let alone what the staff had thought about him. Or a member of the staff's family— most of whom he'd never so much as met or heard about.

Yet here he was, being eaten up by the

thought that the housekeeper's daughter might think he was a jerk.

The housekeeper's daughter—that had been Tanya's sticking point last night, that he couldn't kiss her *because* she was Jo-Beth's daughter. But while that was also what he'd been raised to believe—that there was to be no fraternizing with the help and, certainly, not with the help's daughter—he was wondering now if Tanya had only used that as an excuse. If the real reason had been that she didn't think much of him and so didn't want him kissing her. Or doing anything that might make things more personal between them. If the real reason was that her opinion of him was that low....

Oh, yeah, he definitely hated that thought. It was actually something he'd considered to be a possibility earlier, too—when she'd slipped and let him know she thought he'd lived his life wrapped in cotton he'd had the impression that she didn't think too highly of him then—but he liked it even less now.

So much less that he decided he couldn't just let it slide. He was going to have to talk to her about it. And if that meant trotting out details of his and Katie's private relationship to the help's daughter?

He knew no one would approve of that.

But this was his business and it was important to him.

Although why it was so important he still wasn't sure.

He wasn't sure why it was so important. He wasn't sure if he should let anything personal develop between them. He wasn't sure what was going on with him when it came to Tanya.

He was only sure of one thing—that kissing her last night had been something he'd been wanting to do and denying himself because of his agreement with Katie to go on pretending they were engaged until she gave him the go-ahead to stop. And last night, when he'd been given the go-ahead, kissing Tanya had been uppermost in his mind the whole time they'd been looking at those old family photos.

Only the fact that he *had* kissed her hadn't left him rid of the desire. It had only made him want to kiss her again. And better.

Which she'd told him not to do. And if she'd told him not to do it because she thought he'd been a jerk to Katie, he needed to amend that impression.

Of course if she'd told him not to kiss her again because she just didn't like him...

It was probably better to find that out sooner rather than later.

But simply telling himself that brought back the caring-what-someone-thought-of-him thing.

Because damn it all, housekeeper's daughter or not, he *did* care what Tanya thought of him, and he cared so much it was unsettling.

He'd lost his best friend to war. He'd spent a miserable year himself in the Middle East. He'd come home unable to look at anything the way he had before. But today *this* was what was bothering him?

Regardless of how he tried to dismiss it, though, yes, *this* was what was bothering him. Over and above everything else, he couldn't shed the idea that Tanya Kimbrough, the housekeeper's daughter, might not like him.

That was the long and the short of it.

Unfortunately, coming to that conclusion didn't get him any closer to understanding it.

Or to understanding why it seemed as though Tanya's effect on him was growing by the day....

* * *

"Okay, okay, I get it—the McCords are generous, civic-minded, caring people who have funded, or partially funded, or raised money for, or sponsored innumerable things that all benefit the citizens of Dallas!" Tanya said, crying uncle as Tate pulled into the parking lot of a planetarium that was named for the McCords.

He'd called at one that afternoon to let her know he was back from the hospital. By two they were on a tour of the city. They'd been to the zoo, where the McCords were responsible for a new aviary. They'd been to Meridian Hospital, where an entire surgical suite owed its existence to the prominent family. They'd been to the historical museum, where a new wing was being built by them. They'd driven by two shelters— one for families, another for women and children. They'd been to or driven past a number of other, smaller beneficiaries of the McCord generosity and energies, and it was nearly nine o'clock Wednesday night when they arrived at the planetarium.

"This is where we're having dinner," Tate told her.

"I'm not sure Gummi bears are going to

do it for me," Tanya said. "Besides, I think we're too late—there's only that truck in the lot and the sign says closed."

Tate turned off the engine anyway, giving her that mystery-man smile he flashed to intrigue her. Then he got out.

Tanya wasn't sure what he had up the sleeve of the pale blue shirt he was wearing with a pair of darker blue slacks that fit him like a dream, but she also wasn't sure she was going to go along with it. So she stayed where she was, watching him come around to open her door.

"Honestly," she said from her seat, laying a hand on the notebook she'd been writing in for the last several hours. "I have a complete picture of the McCord good deeds. I don't need to see the stars you provide, too. I'll just add the planetarium to the list, I promise."

He didn't say a word. He merely crooked a long, upturned index finger, motioning for her to get out.

Tanya sighed, took hold of her notebook and pen and complied, hoping he wasn't thinking that snack food at the planetarium was a meal. She'd been so unreasonably excited about seeing him today that she hadn't been hungry for lunch and had literally just waited by the phone for his call. But with only a single pancake to tide her over for the entire day, she was starving and worried that her stomach was going to begin growling at any moment.

Once she was out of the car Tate closed the door and led the way to the planetarium's entrance. When they reached it he didn't even try the door. He just tapped on it—three quick raps of his knuckles.

In answer, it was opened from inside by a man who knew Tate on sight. He said, "Nice to see you, Doctor McCord."

"You, too, Andrew."

The man stepped aside and Tate ushered Tanya in ahead of him, following behind.

Once they were in the planetarium's lobby, Andrew closed the doors and Tate again addressed him. "Are we all set?"

"Yes, sir," the man answered. "You can go right in."

Tate swept an arm toward the theater and that was where he and Tanya went while Andrew quietly brought up the rear as far as the theater doors.

There was already a night sky projected

overhead when Tanya and Tate alone entered the large domed room.

"I give you Paris under a full moon," Tate said then, pointing to the Eiffel Tower silhouetted on the horizon line.

Andrew closed the theater doors, leaving them bathed in the glow of that moon and the dim, milky illumination of the mock streetlights that also dotted the horizon line, surrounding them as if they were on a Parisian avenue.

They were standing in a clear space at the rear of the auditorium seats that descended around the projection platform. Nearby were two chairs positioned at a linen-covered bistro table that was set with china and silver. A small bouquet of white roses and lit candles drew Tanya there just as soft music began to play over the speaker system.

"Wow" was all she said.

Tate joined her at the table. "You'll notice that we have French wine, French bread and French cheeses to start," he said, pointing to the wine that was opened and waiting for them, and at the artfully arranged platter of appetizers. Then he indicated the smaller table nearby and the covered dishes that it held. "When we're ready, we have roasted pork with fennel and herbs, green salad with mustard vinaigrette, flageolet beans with chervil and butter and—for dessert—*pots de crème au chocolat.*"

"Let's start with that," Tanya joked.

"The chocolate?"

"I'm kidding. Sort of…"

He smiled. "We can if you want."

"No. But what are those beans?" she asked, feeling uncultured because she didn't have any idea what they were.

Tate leaned near enough to confide and make her pulse quicken. "I called the best French restaurant I know, took their recommendation and memorized the name but I'd never heard of them before, either. Apparently it's some kind of light-green bean."

Tanya laughed, feeling better about her ignorance, and tried very, very hard not to appear as impressed as she was by all the trouble he'd gone to.

"Is this supposed to be a part of my report?" she asked then.

"The planetarium is. But the dinner is just for us."

"There is no *us,*" she said reflexively, maybe to counteract the fact that she'd liked hearing it.

"There's you. There's me. We have to eat and there's food. We've just put in a full eight-hour workday that's finally finished. And now we can have dinner. That's all there is to it," he assured her.

It didn't seem as if that was all there was to it. It seemed very datelike and incredibly romantic. Which meant that, under the circumstances, she should put up a fuss.

"You wouldn't be trying to compromise my journalistic integrity, would you?" she asked.

"Not my intention."

"What *is* your intention?" she challenged.

He smiled that mystery-man smile once more. "To have dinner after a long day," he insisted, holding out one of the chairs for her.

She still thought he had something up his sleeve but she didn't know what it could be and she *was* starving, and this was all just too appealing for her to turn down.

So she sat in the chair and slipped the linen napkin from the table to the lap of her khaki slacks while Tate went around and took the other chair for himself.

"This *could* actually look bad for you," she goaded him as he poured them both wine and offered her the cheese and bread first.

"Why is that?"

"Well, first you spend the day showing me all the things you and your family do to benefit other people, then you shut down this whole planetarium just to suit yourself. How many small children who need to know where Orion's Belt is for school tomorrow could fail because they came here tonight and found the place closed just for you?"

"It's always closed on Wednesday night," he told her. "And I'm paying Andrew overtime for this, along with getting him seats to some sold-out concert his daughter wants to go to. No one is being hurt, and the only inconvenience is voluntary and well compensated."

"So all in all, today and tonight were to convince me that you're perfect. There are no flaws in the McCords," she teased him slightly as they ate their appetizers and sipped their wine.

"Nobody's perfect. But I know it's easy for people with the kind of life we lead to seem shallow and I wanted to show you that we aren't."

He paused a split second and then said,

"Well, to be honest, shallowness has been true of me to some extent. At least it was. I hope it isn't anymore, and I wanted to be sure it was clear that it isn't the case with the McCords in general."

"Is that why you became a doctor—to stop being shallow?" Tanya asked.

"Actually, it was part of being shallow that *led* me to be a doctor."

"How so?"

"I didn't do it because I was being altruistic or had some higher calling to help humanity," he said as if he disapproved of his own motivation now. "I did it partly because Buzz was going to do it—I told you, his whole family for generations had been in the military, but Buzz didn't want to be in combat. He thought becoming a doctor would give him a better way to do his part. My earliest thought was that I'd give medical school a shot so we could party through that the way we had through college."

"You thought *medical* school was going to be a party?"

"Buzz and I had a knack for making *everything* a party. But my next thought about medicine was that I needed my own thing—Blake had the family business, that was *his* thing. I hated business and didn't want to share his spotlight. So I figured I'd be a doctor—plenty of splash and sparkle and status and respect in that. Then I went all the way to becoming a surgeon because I liked that it was one of the least personal of the specialties—I could stroll in, cut, stroll out."

"That's quite an admission," Tanya said, surprised that he'd made it.

"I don't feel that way now or maybe I wouldn't admit it."

They moved on to their meal with Tate serving her as she said, "You don't regret becoming a doctor, then?"

"No. In fact, I think that if I hadn't, I wouldn't have been able to get through the last year and a half. It's the only thing that's kept me going, that's let me feel as if I could contribute something."

There were two questions that popped into Tanya's mind in response to that. But the most obvious went in the direction of his feelings since his friend's death. And she could already see shadows forming around his mood just at the mention of Buzz, dampening the more lighthearted tone that had followed them through the day and evening. She was loath to explore that and cause those shadows to cover everything. So instead she asked the other question his comment had raised.

"It wasn't Katie who kept you going during the last year and a half?"

Tate shook his handsome head. "Katie is great, don't get me wrong. I think the world of her."

Which was why he'd likely get back with her, Tanya reminded herself to keep this romantic dinner from swaying her too much.

"But the truth is," Tate continued, "what was between Katie and me was just not enough to make Buzz's death any easier."

"Is that why you ended the engagement?" That was private and personal and off-limits for a McCord staff member or a staff member's daughter to ask—again Tanya knew her mother would be appalled. But she was doing it anyway because she just couldn't stop herself. Even though this information was not anything she would include in her story and it was purely her own curiosity that had a hold of her.

"*I* didn't end the engagement," Tate said. "It started out as Katie's idea."

"It *started out* as her idea?"

"It wasn't a big dramatic breakup. There

wasn't a fight or an argument that made her throw the ring in my face, or had me demanding it back. It was like everything has always been between Katie and me—civilized." Tate laughed a wry chuckle. "That was the problem—not a lot of passion. She came to me—when we could work it into our schedules—and said she'd been feeling like our getting married might be a mistake because there *wasn't* any kind of overwhelming passion between us. That we both might deserve more. And I had to agree with her."

"That *is* civilized," Tanya said a bit facetiously, thinking that such civility was reason enough for her not to take the breakup seriously. If Tate and Katie had had a knockdown, drag-out, relationship-killing fight, it might be easier for her to believe they wouldn't get back together. But as it was, this sounded like what she knew of their other breakups—a no-harm, no-foul split that was easily repaired.

"Like I said, there was a shortage of passion. Without it, it's easy to be *civilized,*" Tate said, apparently not offended by her gentle sarcasm. "I think that's also why it didn't upset me to any great degree—once Katie brought it up, not getting married seemed to make more sense than getting married did. I thought she was right—people should get married because they can't stand to be apart, and that was definitely not Katie and me. I just don't want you to think that the engagement ended because I treated Katie badly or dumped her on some kind of stupid whim—"

"Like in the past?" Tanya teased him as he served their desserts.

"We never separated because I treated Katie badly," he defended himself. "That isn't my style."

Tanya smiled, pleased that he seemed so concerned that she might think that of him. She didn't. She knew his success with women had always been in his good treatment of them. But rather than let him off the hook, she said, "But there *were* times when you dumped her on a whim?"

"Katie and I have a long history. Sure, there was a time or two when my reasons for breaking it off with her were pretty shallow—I told you I could be that way before. But to be fair, there was once when Katie dumped me to take a guy with better hair to a country-club dance."

Tanya couldn't imagine anyone with better hair, but she didn't say it. Instead she said, "I don't know, this breakup doesn't sound too much more serious than that."

"It is," Tate insisted as they finished their desserts. "I guarantee that hair was not an issue. I just want you to know that me being some kind of creep *also* wasn't the issue."

Tanya looked more closely at him, seeing just how important it was to him that she not have a negative impression. She was surprised by it.

"Why is what I think such a big deal to you all of a sudden? Even if I refer to you in my report as the family playboy it wouldn't come as news to anyone."

"It's not your *report* that worries me," he said seriously, meeting her eyes to lend weight to his words.

"What *does* worry you?"

He studied her for a moment but somehow in that moment he apparently decided not to answer her question because he smiled a slow, small smile and said, "I'm a little worried right now that maybe you didn't get enough dessert."

Okay, so she *was* trying to spoon out every last creamy drop of that *pots de crème*. She'd just hoped he hadn't noticed.

She smiled sheepishly back at him. "It was fabulous."

Just when Tanya was about to repeat the question he'd dodged, there was a knock on the theater door, and Andrew poked his head in. "The night cleaning crew is here, Doctor McCord."

"Okay, thanks, Andrew," Tate answered. Glancing at Tanya once more he said, "I'm afraid that's our cue—I promised we'd leave so we didn't hold up the cleaning crew."

"Ah, Paris, it was nice while it lasted," Tanya joked as she set her napkin on the table and stood to go.

The opportunity to explore his concerns seemed to have escaped her by the time they got to the car. Tanya used the drive back to the mansion as an opportunity to get a few facts straight about the McCord philanthropies. Then they were home again and Tate was once more walking her to the bungalow's door.

"On Friday night there's a formal dinner, dance and silent auction at the country club—technically, it's a charity ball. Anyway, my family is sponsoring it to raise money for IMC—the International Medical Corps. It's the group I worked with in

Iraq. What do you say to going with me? I'm sure you'll want to sample some of the glitz that goes into being a McCord so you can report on that, too," Tate said as they reached the porch and stepped into the glow of the light her mother had left on for her.

"Formal—as in tuxedos and prom dresses?" Tanya asked.

"I'll be in a tuxedo, yes. But I've never thought of what the women wear as *prom* dresses. Fancy, yes, but—"

"Either way, I don't own anything like that. I'll probably be able to pick up photographs of the event from the society pages to include that element."

"How about this, then," he said as if he didn't intend to take no for an answer. "I have surgeries scheduled all day tomorrow, but what if I take you on a little shopping trip in the evening to outfit you?"

"With a fancy dress?" Tanya said, excited and a little put off by the idea all at once.

"A dress, shoes, whatever it takes to get you there."

"Is this a case of charity beginning at home?" she asked with some distaste.

"Absolutely not. It's a case of my having to go on Friday night because my family initiated it on my behalf. I haven't been doing many of these things since I got back from Baghdad but I have to go to this one and I've been dreading it. Then I started thinking about getting you to go with me, and... no more dread. And since you'd be doing me a favor, it wouldn't be right for you to have to foot the bill for new clothes to do it."

Memories of peeking through the bushes as a child and seeing McCord women dressed in elaborate gowns, the men in tuxedos, flashed through Tanya's mind. It had seemed more like a fantasy than anything real and while some of the events had been held at the mansion, she'd always wondered what the ones held at other places were like.

And now Tate was offering her the opportunity to step into the fantasy.

Actually, he was asking her to do it for him, as a favor.

And it *would* be something she could use for her story....

"Say yes," he urged as if he knew she was weakening. "I'll call and make sure there's an endless supply of *pots de crème* there just for you."

That made her laugh.

"An insider's look," he reminded, "that's

what you signed on for. Friday night will be that."

"Okay…" she said tentatively because she really wasn't sure this was a good idea.

Tentative or not, it was enough to make him smile. "Great!"

"But the only thing I'll accept from you is advice on a dress. I'll buy it myself," she added, her pride taking the forefront.

"No way," he said firmly. "You're doing me the favor, so the dress is my treat."

Pride notwithstanding, as the image of the kind of gowns she'd seen worn for these events became clearer in her mind, she began to fear she might be biting off more than she could chew financially. But rather than completely concede yet, she said, "I'll make a deal with you. Tomorrow I'll call the station and see if they'll buy the dress as a business expense. If they won't—"

"Then you'll let me. Deal. But either way, keep tomorrow night open for shopping."

An evening of shopping for a fairy-tale gown with Tate—as much as Tanya told herself she was wading into risky waters, she couldn't help the little thrill that went through her at the prospect.

"All right, all right, all right," she said as

if she were conceding to something against her will.

And then there was no more to be said except good-night. Only she discovered that she wasn't eager to end her time with him despite the fact that there had been several hours of it.

Maybe he felt the same way because he didn't seem in any hurry to go. She did have the sense that he had something else on his mind, though. She just couldn't guess what it was.

Then, in a hushed voice that let her know that what he was confiding wasn't easy for him to reveal, he said, "Since Buzz died, since coming back from Iraq, things haven't been the same for me. They haven't been as... I don't know, as much fun, I guess. Then I found you in the library Friday night and..." He shrugged. "Things are somehow looking better and better...."

Tanya didn't know what *things* he was talking about but before she could ask, he added, "I can't stand the idea that you might think the worst of me when you seem more and more like the best thing that's happened to me in a long time...."

"It makes a difference what the house-keeper's daughter thinks of you?" she asked.

"It makes a difference what *you* think about me," he said, staring deeply into her eyes.

Then he leaned forward and it was obvious he wanted to kiss her. But rather than doing it, he waited, poised, giving her the chance not to let it happen.

And she knew she shouldn't let it happen. She'd even told him point-blank the night before not to do it again.

But there he was, the man who—in the last few days—had let her see past the charm, the arrogance, the entitlement she'd known of him before, into the vulnerable part of him now. There he was, his starkly chiseled face only inches above hers, *wanting* to kiss her. And she wanted him to.

So she didn't say no. She didn't even shake her head. She just tipped her chin....

It was go-ahead enough.

Tate came the rest of the way, pressing his mouth to hers in a kiss that wasn't quick or brief or offhand like the one the night before. It was a thoughtful, studied kiss with lips parted just slightly and his breath warm and sweet against her skin. It was a kiss that lasted long enough for Tanya to kiss him in return—heaven help her....

Then it ended and Tate straightened to his full height again, smiling a soft, quiet smile.

"Tomorrow night," he said.

Tanya merely nodded and watched him turn and walk away because she was still a little stunned at the thought that he'd just allowed her a glimpse of himself that was unveiled, undisguised.

And that it was that man—the man behind the McCord veneer—who had kissed her....

Chapter Eight

"You're not Cinderella, Tanya."

"I know, Mama." Tanya had probably told her mother more than she should have. She hadn't told her about how Tate had been uncommonly open with her at the end of the previous evening or about the kiss. But she *had* told JoBeth about the charity ball and the dress she was scheduled to go out and shop for with Tate in twenty minutes.

"You're not Cinderella and Tate McCord isn't Prince Charming—or even Doctor Charming—who will whisk you away to the castle to live happily ever after. Not that you *couldn't* be whisked away to something wonderful," her mother added. "It's just that I would want you whisked away to something wonderful by someone better for you than a McCord."

That made Tanya's hairbrush pause in midstroke. "*Better* than a McCord?" she said as she went on to sweep her hair into a twist up the back of her head, leaving curls to cascade at her crown. "I thought you were the McCords' biggest fan."

"I am. But so much money and power sometimes brings the weight of the world down on their shoulders—like Tate seems to be feeling now. It makes them complicated people with complicated lives. And sometimes all that leads them to look outside of their own circle to escape for a while. But not forever, Tanya. Never forever. I've been around here long enough, I have eyes and ears, I know what goes on. And they always end up right back in the middle of that circle. With the same people who have always been there...."

"I know, Mama," Tanya repeated. "I'm going to the charity ball to see firsthand what goes on in that circle of theirs for my report. I have to let Tate pay for the dress because the station I work for doesn't have that kind of budget, and *I* certainly can't afford it. But afterward I'll have the dress cleaned, wrap it up and give it back to him. And I'm not letting any of this go to my head. I promise."

JoBeth didn't look reassured as she stood in the doorway of Tanya's bedroom watching Tanya zip the side zipper of the short-sleeved, black-and-white-checked sundress she'd opted to wear because it was easy to get on and off when she tried on gowns.

It was also extremely formfitting and boosted her breasts just a little above the scoop neck. But it was the easy on-and-off that had made her choose it, not the hint of cleavage it exposed. Or so she told herself....

"Don't let it go to your head, don't let it go anywhere else, either," JoBeth cautioned. "It's dangerous for you to start wanting to live the way they live. To want what they have. To want to be one of them..."

"Everyone wants what they have and to live the way they live—that's why their every move makes news. But I *don't* want to be *one* of them."

"It's even more dangerous to want one of them for yourself. Or to want one of them to want you..."

"I don't want that, either," Tanya swore as she applied a light dusting of blush, a second layer of mascara and some lip gloss to finish getting ready.

When she had—and with Tate due any minute—she grabbed her purse and went to meet her mother face-to-face at the bedroom doorway, uncertain if JoBeth was going to go on blocking it or let her through.

"It's just a job, Mama," Tanya said. "Work. A news report I'm doing. When I have all the material I need I'll go my way and Tate will go his, and that will be it."

Her mother stared at her, frowning.

But when the doorbell rang and they both knew it was Tate there to pick Tanya up, JoBeth did step back and let Tanya out.

Tanya kissed her mother's cheek as she went around her and said, "Don't wait up—I know you have an early day tomorrow." Then she headed for the front door.

And as she did, she thought that she might have just lied a little when she'd told her mother that she didn't want Tate for herself.

She was definitely *trying* not to want him—that much was true.

But was she succeeding?

Almost not at all…

* * *

Shopping McCord-style was not like any other shopping Tanya had ever done. Tate didn't take her to a mall or a department store where there were racks or shelves or displays of clothes for her to pick from. He took her to a shop she'd never even heard of called Dana and Delaney's.

From the outside it looked more like a well-appointed doctor's office and even when they went inside they were welcomed by a woman who stood and came out from behind an antique reception desk to greet Tate by name.

After amenities were exchanged and Tanya was introduced, she and Tate were taken to a private sitting room where they were handed over to Hildy, their fashion advisor.

Hildy invited them to sit on the plush velvet settee, offered them glasses of champagne and then presented them with an array of the kind of gowns Tanya had only seen for herself when spying on McCord social events—all of them a very long way from prom dresses.

Tanya narrowed the field down to five and then she and Hildy adjourned to an

equally elaborate dressing room to try on
the gowns. She refused to model them for
Tate and chose for herself which she liked
best, accepting Hildy's confirmation that the
ruby-red silk taffeta strapless gown that followed her every curve in perfectly petaled
tiers to the floor was The One.

Tanya took Hildy's recommendation for
shoes and a matching clutch, stood still
while the seamstress pinned it for alterations and hemming and then was assured
the dress would be delivered to the McCord
mansion the next afternoon. Never did she
get so much as an inkling of how much she'd
spent, even when Tate instructed Hildy to
have the bill sent to his office. But whatever the ensemble had cost, Tanya had never
worn anything as sophisticated or elegant
and was as excited to wear it again as she
had been to wear her Halloween costumes
as a small child.

Since Tate hadn't been able to pick her up
until nearly eight o'clock, it was after eleven
by the time they left Dana and Delaney's—
long after the shop had closed to the public
or anyone else who didn't receive the special attention allotted the McCords. But just
when Tanya was silently lamenting the fact

that the evening would end so soon, Tate said, "I was in one surgery after another all day and never had a chance to eat—I'm starving. Are you hungry?"

"No, but I don't mind if you want to stop and have something." In fact, she was far more pleased with the prospect of tacking on any amount of time she could to this evening than she should have been, but she didn't let it show.

Tate chose a small sandwich shop only blocks from home. Tanya declined a sandwich but didn't require much persuasion to agree to a warm chocolate chip cookie and a glass of iced tea.

They took the food to a booth in the rear of the deserted restaurant and sat down.

"So," Tate said as he unwrapped his sandwich, "when we were thirteen Buzz and I wanted to learn to surf."

Tanya had no idea where that remark had come from but assuming he was merely making conversation, she said, "Uh-huh…"

"After school one day we decided to practice down the entrance stairs. Dumb idea, I know. Of course it didn't work, my surfboard got away from me and went through a window. Your mom never said a word—

she had the mess cleaned up and the glass replaced before my parents got home and they never knew anything had happened. But the look your mother gave me..." Tate shook his head. "She didn't have to say anything. I knew better than to ever try that in the house again. How come she was giving me that same look from behind you when I picked you up tonight?"

Ah, *that* was where this was going....

Tanya didn't see any reason to beat around the bush. "She's worried about me seeing so much of you."

"Am I a bad influence?" he half joked as he took a bite of his sandwich.

"Yes," she said with a laugh. "But that's not what Mama is upset about. There was a time—I was seven or eight—when my mother realized that I was pressing my nose up against the window of the McCord life, so to speak, and dreaming that that was where I belonged. Mom wanted to snap me out of it to make sure I knew that your lifestyle wasn't the reality for me. Or for most people. But now she's afraid I might slip back into the fantasy again if I hang out with you too much."

"How did she snap you out of it?" he asked.

Tanya smiled slightly—as much at the thought of her mother's wisdom as at the sight of his angular features shadowed by a hint of the beard he apparently hadn't had the chance to shave between surgery and getting her to the dress shop. It made him look rugged and scruffily handsome and so sexy that it did make him a danger to her—dangerously attractive....

"How did my mother snap me out of it...." Tanya repeated because she'd been a little lost in admiring him and needed to catch up. "She sent me to the real world," she said.

"*Real* people, *real* world—I think I'm detecting a theme," he joked.

Tanya didn't respond to that. She merely went on explaining how her mother had focused her. "The way you live may be the real world for you, but it isn't the real world for most people—the world that my mom knew I would have to live and work and function and survive in—and it was important to her that I be aware of that. So she started to send me for most weekends, holidays and vacations to stay with my grandparents whether she could get away or not."

"I take it your grandparents *do* live in the real world?"

"They're regular working people—before they retired my grandfather was in construction, my grandmother was an elementary school custodian. And I saw firsthand through them what I didn't see living with my mom inside the walls of your world even if I wasn't a part of your world."

"What did you see?" Tate asked as if he were genuinely interested.

"I saw firsthand what it was like for people to have to stretch a dollar to make ends meet when they didn't have leftovers from the McCord kitchen to supplement their groceries, for one," she said, trying not to bask in the intensity of his interest in her at that moment—even though it *was* nice to have such undivided attention from him…. "I saw firsthand what can happen when someone gets hurt on the job and loses income," she continued. "I saw how medical expenses can cost people their savings, their house, everything, and how those people might not know where to turn—"

"Did that happen to your grandparents?" he asked with what sounded like alarm.

"Some of it. Some happened to their

good friends, to their next-door neighbors who ended up having to move in with their son when hard times hit. It was all heart-wrenching no matter who it was happening to. I just saw what it is to live the life *I* was born to, not the life you were. My grandparents also made sure I knew things my mom had protected me from—"

"Such as?"

"How hard it had been for Mama to have my father walk out on her and leave her with a kid and no child support. My mom didn't want to burden me with her own problems, and I was only two when my father took a hike, so my earliest memories are of living in the housekeeper's cottage, playing in your kitchen or on the grounds of your house while my mother worked. I didn't have any idea what my mom had been through or how tough it had been for her, or how easy it was for a man to dump his family, not support his kid and get away with it."

Tate had finished eating and he wadded up his sandwich wrapper. But then he sat back, laid a long arm across the back of the bench on his side of the booth and seemed in no hurry to move on. Instead, his attention was still on her, studying her.

"It's strange, it seems as if you've always been around and because of that I thought I knew you—*some,* anyway. But I really don't, do I?"

"I guess you're getting to," Tanya pointed out. "Although I don't know why knowing me would be one of your priorities."

"Because you're an interesting person?"

"Oh, I know," she said facetiously, laughing. "I'm fascinating."

Tate ignored that. He went on watching her as if she was intriguing him regardless of what she thought. "So your mom sent you out to learn what the real world is like but now she's thinking you might get sucked into my world after all?"

"Into wanting to be a part of your world," Tanya amended. "What she doesn't realize is that since she made sure I *did* grow up seeing the real world, I also grew up feeling strongly that I should do something to shine a light on all the things that make the real world harder for people."

"That's why you went into the news business?"

"I'll grant you that it isn't saving someone's life on an operating table. Or doing the everyday work at the shelters—although I have volunteered and will again once I'm completely settled in in Dallas again. But through broadcast journalism I have the chance to air wrongs when I find them, to announce to a whole lot of people at once that there's help to be had and where to find it. I believe that that kind of guidance, that kind of exposure can make things change—"

"Exposure can make people change all right," Tate said, again as if it held meaning for him.

But before Tanya could explore it, he said, "A story about a rare diamond is hardly shining a light on the plight of the working man, though."

"Or the working woman," she added. "But I'm hoping it's my ticket to a position where that's what I can do. As it is now, standing in an ice storm reporting on slick roads doesn't make much of a difference. The diamond, the McCords, the feud with the Foleys—I'm just hoping it will earn me an anchor chair where I can do more."

Those clear, sky-blue eyes of his seemed to be boring into her. "I admire that drive to help. And you for being so determined."

That was gracious. And cordial. It wasn't

you're so hot I can hardly stand not to pull you under this table right now and make you mine. But it still should have been gratifying.

And definitely the way things *should* have been between them.

It was just that she felt slightly disappointed by the impersonal sentiment it seemed to convey.

"It's not admirable, it's just why I became what I became and what I'm trying to do," she said. "It's also probably more than you wanted to hear and boring you to tears."

It was her own misplaced dejection that she was dodging when she gathered up the debris of his dinner and her own dessert and took it to the trash. She just didn't want to want anything more personal from him. She didn't want to want him....

And she had to nip it in the bud.

"We should probably get going," she announced when she returned to the table and found Tate still sitting where he had been before.

"It wasn't more than I wanted to hear," he said as if she'd just made that comment. "Why? Because you're trying to get in touch with your employees and their families?"

She knew she was doing the same thing she had the night he'd told her he wasn't engaged anymore—being curt and somewhat abrasive to protect herself, to put distance between them.

But tonight he didn't seem to let it get to him. Very patiently, he said, "One thing I *never* am when I'm with you, Tanya, is bored. I like talking to you. Listening to you. Being with you."

Oh, that just made it worse....

"You don't have to—"

He laughed. "No one said I did. I just do."

He did stand, however, motioning toward the door to let her know he'd leave because she'd made it so obvious that was what she was ready to do.

As he opened the shop door and then the passenger door of his car for her he said, "I'm betting the next thing you're going to say is that the only reason we're spending time together is for your job, and that's what we need to do—get back to business."

That *had* been what she was going to say. Basically.

"Well, my mom was right about tonight—

it would be hard to sell what we've been doing as work."

"Think of it as being fitted for your uniform and then taking a lunch hour," he said wryly before he closed her door and went around to get in behind the wheel.

It was a short drive home and neither of them said anything during the trip.

Tanya had no idea what was on Tate's mind as he drove, but she was trying like mad not to be as aware as she was of every little detail—from the faint scent of his cologne, to the way his longish hair grazed the collar of his shirt, to his big, masculine hands on the steering wheel.

Her mother was right, she kept telling herself. To him, she was nothing but a brief stepping-outside-of-his-circle that he seemed to need right now. When that need passed, he'd go back inside the circle. Without her. And likely *with* Katie Whitcomb-Salgar.

No matter what he said....

When they got home Tate didn't immediately get out of the car. After turning off the engine he pivoted and stretched his arm across the top of her seat the way he'd been sitting at the restaurant, and said, "I have to make rounds in the morning but I'll be home by noon or so. Would you like to use the afternoon for Foley feud facts and diamond lore?"

The way he said that made Tanya smile in spite of herself. "Okay."

"When would you like to do it?"

Without thinking about it, she'd angled in her seat, too, and was looking at his traffic-stopping face and supple mouth, and suddenly remembering all too vividly that kiss of the night before.

"Why don't you come to the cottage?" she suggested. "Mama said she has electricians stringing the lights for the Labor Day party around the pool and the grounds tomorrow. The caterers are coming to put the final touches on the menu, and I think the tent people might be starting the set-up on top of everything else. So it seems like there will be too much going on to get any work done in the middle of all that."

"You know more about what's happening at my house than I do."

"That's my mother's job," she reminded him. "But if you come to the cottage I'll make lunch and we can sit on the patio back here, away from the fray."

Tate smiled a slow smile. "You're going to make me lunch?"

"It's the least I can do since you keep buying me dinner…and tonight's cookie. Don't expect anything fancy—just something we can munch on while you tell me about the skeletons in the McCord closet."

"Ah, yes, the skeletons…" he said with a comical wiggle of his eyebrows.

But even with their plans for the next day set, he didn't move. He merely went on looking at her for a moment longer before he said, "I keep wondering if things would be different if you and I had just met. If I was just Joe Somebody and you were just Fledgling Newscaster, and our paths crossed—"

"You mean if you weren't a *McCord* and a member of the family that employs my mother, and I wasn't the housekeeper's daughter?" Another reminder to him.

"If we maybe met in the E.R. when you had a hot appendix that I had to remove—"

"Or we could meet because I was doing a story on up-and-coming surgeons in Dallas— at least then no blood would have to be spilled."

He laughed. "Okay, no blood. But then if I asked about your background, your family, where you grew up, you'd just think I wanted to know."

"No excess baggage," Tanya said.

"It might be nice…."

"Mmm," she agreed, thinking that it would be very, very nice. And make all of this so much different.

"Would you spend time with me then, just because I asked you to?" he probed.

"Not if your goal was to cut me open," she joked because she was leery of admitting too much.

"How about if my goal was just to be with you? Would you give me a chance?"

Should she lie and say no? Or should she go out on a limb with the truth?

"I'd probably give you a chance," she said tentatively. "But that isn't how things are."

He moved his hand from the back of her seat to her nape, toying with the stray wisps of hair that were free of the twist that held the rest, sending goose bumps down her spine.

"Still," he said, "if we'd have a chance under different circumstances, it seems as if we should have a chance under these."

"Different circumstances would change things," she said, wondering how her voice could have been so soft when she'd wanted it to be firm.

He nodded, agreeing with her. But as his eyes held hers she didn't have the sense that he completely concurred. "It's hard to care about circumstances, sometimes, when they seem so far removed from what's here and now...."

"They aren't *so* far," Tanya said with a glance in the direction of the bungalow.

"Seems pretty far," he nearly whispered, compelling her to look at him again, to let him peer into her face, search her eyes with his.

His hand went from her nape to brush her cheek with the backs of his fingers and it felt so good she knew she should run. That she should open that car door, get out and just plain flee before this went any further.

But she didn't. Instead, somewhere along the way, she'd tipped her head into his caress.

She tipped it enough so that when he leaned forward to press his mouth to hers, she didn't even have to make an adjustment for it to happen.

And then there they were, kissing again. With a little familiarity tonight. With lips that were parted, with breath mingled, and nothing else seemed to matter from the moment it began.

Tate's hand returned to the back of her neck, cradling her head as he deepened the kiss, as his lips parted even more.

His other hand came to the side of her face then, while his mouth opened wider and his tongue made an appearance. Just the tip at first, testing the inner edge of her teeth, urging her to give him more leeway so he could meet and greet her tongue.

And her tongue seemed to have a mind of its own when he did, because the very second it encountered his it was just plain wanton. She gave as good as she got, every bit as adroitly, as adeptly, as aggressively until mouths were open wide and that kiss had turned wild and untamed.

Mouths clung and his arms came around her and pulled her to him. She let hers circle him, too, her breasts straining for his chest, their tips only barely finding him in the awkwardness of being separated by a gearshift. If only he'd waited until he'd walked her to the door tonight!

But then her mother might have seen this....

The thought of her mother cooled things for Tanya. Even though there was nothing in her that wanted it cooled. Even though everything in her was urging her on to more.

But this time her reminder was to herself—these weren't different circumstances. He wasn't Joe Somebody. Things were what they were and losing sight of that was not wise.

Tanya slipped her arms from around him and pressed her hands against his chest to push just enough to let him know this couldn't go on.

And yet she didn't push so much that she ended the kiss, it was Tate who had to do that—in stages, slowly, reluctantly.

But he did it, sighing softly when he had.

"We need to remember—" Tanya said, her voice a much sexier whisper than it should have been "—that I'm the housekeeper's daughter and that you're—"

"The guy who doesn't want any of that to matter."

"But it does," Tanya insisted.

He shook his head, denying it, but still Tanya moved the rest of the way away from him to make it clear she meant what she said.

"Don't walk me to the door," she commanded because in her mind she could see them there—him kissing her again, her up against him in a seamless meeting of their bodies while mouths renewed what she was craving so much she could hardly stand it. She knew it would only make it more difficult to put the brakes on again. "Call me when you leave the hospital tomorrow so I'll know when to expect you," she added just before she opened the car door and left Tate behind. All without another word from him, only a frown that said he didn't like that she was going.

But Tanya went anyway, not glancing back, making a beeline for her mother's tiny house, feeling Tate's eyes on her the whole way.

Tate, who would leave and return to his so, so much bigger house.

Where he belonged.

Where she didn't.

But that kiss? When their mouths met it was definitely in some no-man's-land in the middle, between his world and hers.

And as Tanya let herself into her mother's place she couldn't help wishing that there was some way to stake a claim of her own on a little of that no-man's-land.

Where she might actually be able to have something with Tate…

Chapter Nine

"I know I said that I was going to start
my report with your grandfather Harry and
Gavin Foley because the feud began with
them, but after doing more research I think
I have to take it a generation back from
there—at least on the Foley side—to get
the diamond in," Tanya said.

It was Friday afternoon and she and Tate
were sitting at her mother's patio table outside the bungalow's back door. They were
eating shepherd's pie and salads that Tanya
had made. There were also two glasses of
iced tea and a pitcher nearby for refills. But
Tanya was less interested in the food than in

trying to keep her mind off of Tate in order to concentrate on her work.

It wasn't easy. The table was small and even sitting across from each other their knees kept brushing together under it. And every contact caused those same little goose bumps that had gone down her spine when his hand had closed around the nape of her neck last night.

"The Santa Magdalena diamond goes back to Elwin Foley—Gavin's father," Tate supplied, obviously unaware of what merely being near him did to her.

Tanya picked up the story from there, reciting what she'd learned on the Internet. "And it was Elwin who—so the story goes—was sailing on the ship that was possibly a ship of thieves. The ship was carrying the diamond and other treasures of some sort when it went down. Not many of the crew survived but Elwin did, and rumor had it that he somehow made off with the diamond and a jewel-encrusted chest of coins."

"That's what I've always heard," Tate confirmed between bites.

"But according to my research," Tanya continued, "it wasn't verified that anything *but* the few crew members had made it off the ship until divers located the ship a few months ago. When no jewel-encrusted chest of coins and no Santa Magdalena diamond were found on it, the possibility that Foley *could* have made off with them increased."

"Or the diamond and the treasure weren't ever on board in the first place and the whole thing was a tall tale," Tate said.

Tanya had to glance up from her notes to look at him. She'd been trying to avoid too much eye contact because every time it happened she flashed back to that kiss they'd shared in his car the night before and all she really wanted to do was jump the man's bones. But she wasn't going to let him get away with pretending that there was no foundation to any of what she was hoping would be the pinnacle of her report—the Santa Magdalena diamond and its discovery.

"I've read the history of the stone," she said. "It was mined in India. It's a flawless forty-eight-carat canary diamond with perfect clarity, and it's said to be even more beautiful than the Hope Diamond. There's no question that it exists—in case your next move is to try to convince me that even *that* was never any more than legend. There's also no question that the diamond's last known location was on that same ship that Elwin Foley was on. It's now known that the diamond hasn't been at the bottom of the ocean all this time, which means the likelihood that Foley got away with it is all the greater. And since the McCords ended up with the only Foley assets years ago…" Tanya let that conclude itself. But she did add, "And—supposedly—the diamond has also brought only bad luck to any hands it's fallen into and is believed to be cursed. Maybe a curse that's responsible for the Mc-Cord empire hitting its current slump?"

Tate grinned. "Cursed? Now *that* sounds more like myth or folklore than fact."

He was hedging and she knew it as surely as she knew she wanted to run her hands through his hair.

"The cursed part may be myth or folk-lore, but none of the rest of this is," Tanya said, standing her ground. "What you and Blake were talking about on Friday night came through loud and clear in the library— I know that your family is looking for the diamond. And with reason to believe that it can be found. So don't waste my time try-ing to make me think for a minute that we're talking fiction rather than fact."

"You'll never just roll over and make it easy for me, will you?" he said with more of that grin that let her know he liked the challenge.

Had Katie Whitcomb-Salgar not provided that for him? Tanya wondered. Or would not getting his own way with her be what drove him back to the heiress?

Not that it made any difference to Tanya. She wasn't changing her position regardless. Although the image of *rolling over* for him did have its own appeal...

Then Tate said, "I thought we were talking history."

"In other words, let's stick to the safe subject of the past."

Tate's smile turned very Cheshire cat and it was so sexy it blew her away.

She took a bite of her lunch and used the moment to get a grip on herself so she could redevote her attention to her work.

"All right, that's the diamond's background," she said then. "Let's get into the feud and how the McCords became the owners of Foley land and silver mines."

"Fairly," Tate said defensively. "But that's not the way Gavin Foley saw it."

"How did Gavin Foley see it?"

"He and my grandfather—Harry McCord—

were playing poker. Gavin put up the deed to his land and the five mines on it—mines that *his* family had started and never stuck with long enough to make them pay out. Gavin lost, my grandfather won the hand and the deed."

"Fair and square," Tanya said.

"Only Gavin figured he couldn't have lost unless my grandfather cheated. Which he didn't. But Gavin swore to his dying day that the game was fixed."

"His dying day was when?" Tanya asked, taking notes.

"I'm not sure. A while ago—eight, nine, ten years—you'll have to get the exact date from somewhere else if you need it. I know it was after my mother persuaded my father to offer the Foleys the opportunity to lease the land from us."

"Why did your mother do that?"

"She was hoping it would end the feud that started with that card game. It was always Gavin Foley's goal to get back on that land, and while the lease didn't return ownership to him, it did give him the chance to start a ranch there. He was pretty old by then but the family pitched in to start it up for him, and his grandson—Travis—helped him run it until he died. Travis Foley still runs it now."

"But lease or no lease, the feud didn't end?"

Tate shook his head. "The Foleys—being the *Foleys*—took the lease and just went on acting as if we'd done something wrong."

"Did Elwin Foley hide the diamond somewhere on the land? Is that why Gavin was so determined to get back onto it—to look for the stone and the treasure?" Tanya asked.

The Cheshire cat smile came out again. "Do I look like a mind reader? All I know is that Gavin Foley wanted back on the land but getting there through leasing it didn't appease him. He still said the land was rightfully his and he still hated us because it wasn't. He apparently kept his family fired up about it, too, and the lease didn't end the Foleys' dislike of us."

"Or the McCords' dislike of the Foleys," Tanya pointed out.

Tate's only answer was to raise his iced tea glass as if in toast before he took a drink.

"Did the lease essentially give the land back to the Foleys indefinitely?" Tanya asked.

Tate shook his head. "It's a fifty-year lease—it'll be up in thirty years or so—"

"Then—doing the math—your mother pushed for the lease for the Foleys right about the time she was pregnant with your brother Charlie, Rex Foley's son...."

Tate had a mouthful of shepherd's pie when she said that and he chewed very, very slowly, all the while staring at her in a way that made it obvious he hadn't liked her figuring that out.

When he'd swallowed he went on as if she hadn't said it.

"So in thirty years when the lease is up we could just kick Travis off the ranch and the land if we wanted to. And the lease is for the land only—we retained the mineral rights to the mines—the Foleys have no business anywhere near any of them."

Message received—he was not going to talk about his younger brother's parentage.

Since that wasn't her focus today anyway, Tanya conceded and stuck to the subject at hand.

"Are you still taking silver out of the mines?"

"No. It was my family who ended up digging deep enough to actually strike substantial silver. But the five mines themselves were played out years ago. They were the foundation for the jewelry business. Retaining the mineral rights is more on principle than anything. The mines don't do us any good anymore and they wouldn't do the Foleys any good either."

"Besides, the Foleys made their money in oil, didn't they?"

"That they did."

Tanya had barely touched her lunch but Tate was finished with his and sat back in his chair. It didn't help her to now have his penetrating eyes so steadily on her. It did improve her posture, though....

Work—just stick with work, she commanded herself.

"So, I'm not sure I understand how the feud has been fueled over the years," she said. "It seems as if when the Foleys made their own fortune in oil they should have stopped resenting the McCords."

"That's where it gets more personal," Tate said.

"Because of your mother originally dating both your father and Rex Foley?" Tanya guessed, referring to what Tate had told her when they'd looked through his family albums.

"There was definitely bad blood over

that," Tate admitted. "Like I said before, I don't know much about it, but I do know that there was a rivalry that breathed new life into the feud. I also know that my mother dated Rex Foley all through high school and thought he was the man she would marry, and that my father was jealous of that. I don't have any idea what happened for her and Rex to break up, but that was when she got together with my father."

Tanya hesitated, wondering if what she wanted to explore next was going to make Tate angry. But she ventured it despite the risk.

"In my research I made note of some dates. Blake was born less than nine months after your parents married...."

"Is that right?" Tate said but in a way that made it clear it was no news to him.

"So...the union of your parents was a shotgun wedding?"

"I've never been told there were weapons involved. And to be honest, it isn't something I've ever had a heart-to-heart talk about with my mother. I'm sure it isn't something she'd want on the news, though."

Second message received—the advantage of having Tanya do the story was that

that was a tidbit that should be omitted as a courtesy.

But she wasn't interested in doing a sleazy tabloid-type report so Tanya didn't pursue that, either.

She did say, "It's strange, isn't it, how intertwined the Foleys and the McCords are even though you all hate each other? Especially now with Charlie being a Foley…."

Tate gave her that glare again to warn her away from talking about Charlie.

"Okay, I know you're probably protective of him," Tanya said. "I respect that, and I'm not going to put any of that too-personal stuff in, so you can relax."

That must have eased his mind because he seemed to have let down his guard when he said, "You're right, though, about how intertwined we always are with the Foleys. I just found out that Penny is involved with Jason Foley."

"Really?" Tanya said. She had the sense that they had just somehow stopped working, that Tate was actually confiding in her. And being offered that kind of trust from him gave her an entirely new kind of rush.

"That's what Penny said at dinner the other night," he confirmed. "I'm not sure to what extent she's involved with Foley, but you're right, there does always seem to be some *intertwining*."

"Your family can't be happy about a relationship between Penny and a Foley," Tanya observed.

"Definitely not happy about it, no. Decidedly leery of it. Unanimously worried for her. For my part, I'd like to be happy for her but a Foley coming into the picture right now just seems a little *too* convenient to me."

"Right now when it looks as if their ancestor really did get away with the diamond and probably stashed it on the land they lost to you. At a time when the diamond could be up for grabs to the first person to find it," Tanya summarized.

Tate answered only with an arch of his eyebrows.

"Still," Tanya said, "Penny has a lot to offer—it's possible that Jason Foley just likes her, isn't it?"

Tate looked as though he wanted to believe that but wasn't convinced.

There was no opportunity for him to answer her question, however, because just then Edward, the McCords' butler, appeared from around the side of the bungalow carrying a garment bag.

"Excuse me for interrupting. But Tanya, this just arrived from Mrs. McCord's favorite shop. The deliveryman insisted it was for you. I told him he must be mistaken, especially since he also said the bill that goes with it is for you, Doctor McCord. But it *is* your name on the ticket, Tanya, and the envelope is addressed to Doctor McCord. Can that be right?"

And just like that Tanya went from feeling perfectly fine to feeling awkward and uncomfortable and humbled....

"It's right, Edward," Tate said. "The dress is for Tanya. The bill was supposed to go to my office but it's for me regardless. You can leave it on my desk."

Tanya sat there frozen and speechless, looking up at the man who had worked for the McCords as long as her mother had, knowing that reality was staring back at her from his questioning eyes.

She was well aware of what the staff said—and thought—about any employee who foolishly tried to step from the oven or the dust cloth or the garden shears into the McCord family ranks. And as Edward stood there with that garment bag, she knew he was wondering if she had become one of them.

No pride, no dignity, no brains because it never actually happened—that was what was said of those who hadn't known their place and had attempted to climb that particular social ladder.

Now, for sure, there would be gossip about her, whispers. Her mother would be embarrassed to have to admit that Tate McCord had bought her a dress that likely cost more than any one of the staff earned in a month's salary. And Tanya wanted to crawl into a hole and hide from the shocked expression of a man she was fond of and respected and didn't want thinking badly of her.

But sitting there like a statue wasn't helping anything so she got up to take the garment bag.

"Thanks, Edward," she muttered as she did, unable to meet him eye to eye, wishing she could say *it isn't what you think.* Suffering some guilt over the fact that the kisses she and Tate had shared didn't make her altogether innocent, either....

"I'll leave this other on your desk, Doctor," Edward said then, leaving.

For Tanya there was so much tension in the air it seemed palpable, but if Tate picked up on it, it didn't show. And he didn't have a chance to say anything because his cell phone rang just then.

"It's one of my nurses, I'll have to take this," he said after checking the display. Then he flipped the phone open to answer it.

While he did, Tanya gave him some privacy by carrying the garment bag into the house.

In spite of the negatives that had just come of it, once she'd hung the bag over the top of the pantry door she couldn't resist unzipping the zipper to look at the dress.

It was even more beautiful than she remembered. Too beautiful to have caused such ugly feelings.

But now there were both the negatives and the positives churning inside of her.

"I have to go back to the hospital—"

Tanya jumped at the sound of Tate's voice coming from behind her where he was poking his head through the screen door. "One of my patients is having some problems. But I should be back in time for tonight."

Tanya nodded, thinking that as she stood there, with the beautiful dress on one side and Tate's handsome face on the other, it just seemed so unfair that there had to be any negatives at all.

But the lingering sense that she was somehow doing something to be ashamed of remained just the same.

"Thanks for lunch," Tate said then.

"You're welcome," Tanya answered even as doubt washed over her about whether she should wear the dress and go with him tonight.

Or stay at home in the housekeeper's bungalow with her mother.

Where she belonged…

Tanya and what they'd talked about over lunch was still on Tate's mind as he drove to the hospital.

He'd made sure he told her only what wouldn't do any harm for her to know, what was common knowledge. He hadn't told her that at about the same time the sunken ship had been discovered and it was confirmed that the diamond wasn't on it, Blake had been going through their father's personal papers hoping for ideas to help boost the business. In the process of that, Blake had found the deed their grandfather had won from Gavin Foley.

Tate hadn't told Tanya that in looking at that deed, Blake's memory had been triggered from his boyhood spent exploring those played out mines on the land. That Blake had realized that there could well be a clue in the drawings that decorated the deed's border. That the mines themselves were each marked by a stone bearing a petroglyph of its name—the Turtle mine, the Eagle, the Bow, the Lizard, the Tree— and that images of those petroglyphs were drawn on the border.

Tate hadn't told Tanya that all but one of the drawings were identical to the petroglyphs that Blake knew well. But that in the drawing of the eagle there was a diamond in the bird's talons. A diamond that wasn't on the petroglyph itself.

Tate certainly hadn't told Tanya that because of that one tiny discrepancy, Blake was banking on the Santa Magdalena diamond and the treasure chest of coins being hidden in the Eagle mine. Or that Blake had enlisted their sister Paige to secretly find the diamond—which she was about to try to do—in the deserted mine that was now a part of the ranch the McCords had leased to Travis Foley.

It wasn't that he wouldn't give Tanya all of that information when the diamond and the treasure were safely in McCord hands—in fact he was hoping it would make not only a career-building revelation for her, but would generate the publicity McCord's Jewelers needed to rebound from the current slump. He just couldn't tell her any of that now.

He also hadn't gotten into the more personal aspects of his family's history, but those he might never give her. He certainly wasn't going to tell her that not only had his mother been pregnant with Blake when she'd married his father, but that it was relatively clear to the whole family that their parents' marriage had never been a love match. Or that his mother had always treated Blake differently, that she'd never seemed to bond with him the way she had with Tate, the twins or certainly with Charlie, whom she doted on.

That was just not information that needed airing.

And yet he *had* told her about Penny and Jason Foley....

Not that he'd told her that with any fore-thought—the words had just come out.

His sister being involved with a Foley had been weighing on him and he'd felt the urge to get it off his chest. And all of a sudden he had. To Tanya.

But not in terms of giving her information for her news report. Just because she was who he'd felt inclined to tell. The one person he'd had the urge to open up to. The first person since Buzz...

Was he honestly finding similarity between his relationship with Tanya and his friendship with Buzz?

That didn't seem possible.

And yet there *was* something similar in how easy it was to be with Tanya. To be himself with her.

Of course the other things she stirred in him couldn't have been more *un*like his friendship with Buzz. But still, what was there about Tanya that seemed to draw him out of himself?

He couldn't explain it even after trying for several miles to figure it out.

He just knew that he liked the way he felt when he was with her.

More than liked it—he was beginning to crave it.

And it was over and above the fact that he liked her. That he craved her in so many other ways....

But liking her, craving time with her, craving *her,* was all there, too. And growing so much, so fast that last night's sleeplessness had been solely due to that kiss ending too soon and forcing him to go home more frustrated than he'd been since puberty.

And all through lunch today? He might have been talking poker games and lost diamonds and feuds, but what he'd been thinking about was the reddish streaks glistening in her shiny hair. About the way her skin turned nearly translucent in the sunshine. About how natural light let him see tiny lines of topaz in her dark eyes. And how when she sat up straight her breasts pressed against her tank top the way he'd wanted them pressed against him last night.

What he'd been thinking about was how he'd just wanted to pull her over that table and onto his lap and kiss her again....

That had been about when Edward had shown up with the dress.

Everything had changed then.

Tanya had seemed so uncomfortable. So self-conscious. Her face had turned the color of the stoplight he was paused at at this very moment.

Did she think the butler was judging her? Disapproving?

Was Edward judging her?

The butler hadn't liked that the dress did belong to Tanya or that Tate had paid for it—Tate *had* gotten that impression. And as for disapproving? There had been that, too, he thought.

Damn.

He regretted that he'd inadvertently put Tanya in that position.

So take her out of it, he told himself.

But taking her out of the position she was in meant delegating her back to the staff side of things while he stayed firmly on the other side of the line that divided them.

And while he knew intellectually that that was probably what he *should* do, he also knew he couldn't. Not when it could cost him nights like last night and afternoons like today. Not when it would cost him having Tanya by his side tonight at the damn charity ball he didn't want to go to.

Because the only thing that was making

him look forward to tonight was the thought that he was going to be with her.

And more than that, what was helping him to increasingly see daylight through the darkness was Tanya.

And he just couldn't give that up.

At least not before he had to…

Chapter Ten

Everything about Friday evening fell just short of being perfect.

Tanya's dress was even more fabulous than she remembered it—or maybe it was the minor alterations that had made it even better. Her hair worked exactly the way she wanted it to—it was just full enough, just wavy enough, and it cascaded around her shoulders just the way she wanted it to. She did on-camera makeup to make sure she didn't look washed-out, and yet the only thing her mother said when JoBeth took in the complete picture was a very flat, "You look nice," before reminding Tanya that she didn't think this was a good idea and warning her to be careful in a tone as dire as she might have used if Tanya was about to walk through a field of land mines.

Not the most perfect of send-offs.

When Tate picked her up he seemed duly impressed by his initial look at her—his eyebrows shot up, he breathed an appreciative breath that would have blown out a birthday candle and said, "Wow!" And he looked dashing and sophisticated in a black peak-lapel tuxedo with a shadow stripe, a white shirt and a tie that was also white but with a silver cast to it.

Yet there was something subdued about him that Tanya thought was an example of what her mother and the rest of the staff had said about his recent moods—he was quieter than he'd been at any time since he'd discovered Tanya in the library a week ago, and he seemed somehow removed, distant.

Again, not quite perfect.

The charity ball was everything Tanya had imagined as a child. The country club's ballroom was large and elegantly decorated. Crystal chandeliers hung overhead. The tables were linen covered and set with fine china and silver and adorned with an abundance of roses.

The women were all dressed impeccably in gowns as fine as Tanya's, the men in tuxedos as well tailored as Tate's. There was subtle music being played by a twelve-piece orchestra, and the food was some of the best Tanya had ever eaten. Tate introduced her to more people than she could keep track of, and Tanya was relieved that his former fiancée hadn't yet returned to Dallas and so wasn't there.

His family was courteous and friendly in an awkward sort of way. But despite the fact that not everyone knew she was the housekeeper's daughter, at no time during the evening did Tanya feel warmly welcomed into Tate's social circle. Instead, she was acutely aware of the fact that she was a fish out of water. It made her wonder if she should have let the afternoon's doubts prevail over her desire to be with Tate.

Once more, not exactly perfect.

And maybe that had as much to do with Tate as it did with Tanya's acceptance— or lack of it—with his peers. Because all through the evening she continued to be aware of that "something different" about him that she couldn't completely pinpoint. Or explain.

He was flawlessly attentive and considerate of her, but he was somber and he made only minimal effort to mingle with anyone else. Plus he seemed barely able to tolerate the many, many people who approached him to welcome him home from the Middle East, to applaud him for the year he'd spent there, to let him know they were happy to be contributing to his cause. It was as if with each time that happened, Tate became more stiff, and Tanya could sense the tension in him was growing.

So no, not quite the perfect evening.

After dinner and several people taking the podium to applaud Tate for his war efforts and to talk about the silent auction and where the proceeds would go, the orchestra began playing music to dance to. That was when Tate leaned close to Tanya's ear and said, "My family will stay to the end but I think my obligations here are about done. Would you mind if we cut this short and left?"

Because it *wasn't* quite the perfect evening, Tanya assured him that she wouldn't mind at all and let him guide her from the ballroom without a backward glance.

On the drive home she was still trying to figure out what was going on with him so once they were well on their way she said, "That patient you had to go back to the hospital for today—did they do okay?"

"Fine," he answered, still sounding as if his mind was elsewhere. "He just needed an increase in his pain meds."

"And what about you? Do you feel okay?"

"I'm fine, too," he said without taking his eyes off the road.

But he didn't offer her any more than that and in this mood, she was slightly wary of pushing him. She left him to his silence, recalling what her mother had said about the McCords having the weight of the world on their shoulders. Looking at Tate and how troubled he seemed, Tanya thought her mother might be right.

Tonight when they reached the estate Tate pulled up to the front of the main house rather than going nearer to the housekeeper's bungalow.

He still didn't say anything and had opened her door by the time Tanya had gathered her purse and tugged on her skirt to make sure she didn't catch a heel in the hem when she got out.

Then Tate closed a strong hand around her elbow and steered her through the mansion's front door.

It was not a door Tanya had gone through more than a few times in her life, and never with a McCord. And it made her think that he really *was* distracted.

Maybe he'd forgotten where she lived. Or that she *wasn't* Katie Whitcomb-Salgar.

Or maybe tonight he was so enmeshed in his own doldrums that it was just up to her to make her way through the house and let herself out the back to get home on her own....

But once they were inside, Tate took a right turn at the far end of the foyer and suddenly Tanya found herself in the den with only a single desk light on to cast a dim glow in the large room.

"How about a drink?" he asked.

Tanya had had champagne at the ball, while Tate had nursed nothing but sparkling water. "I get sick if I mix liquors so I think I'll pass. But you go ahead—you haven't had anything all night."

He just shook his head as if he'd changed his mind and a drink didn't appeal to him after all.

Then he surprised her by taking her hand and giving her an endearingly shamefaced smile. "Come and sit with me and let me apologize to you," he said, pulling her along with him to the sofa.

Every other time he'd touched her throughout the evening it had been the lightest of contacts—on her back, her arm—all absolutely appropriate and proper, and still each one had set off those goose bumps again. But none of it had been anything like the warmth that flooded her at having his big hand close completely around hers as if it was something he'd done a million times before.

She tried not to let it be such a big deal to her.

But then they reached the couch and after urging her to sit he released her hand and she felt disappointment.

There was some compensation for the loss in watching him shrug out of his tie, though, and toss it aside. In watching him open his collar button as if he needed air and take off the tuxedo jacket—rolling the tension out of his broad shoulders in a way that made her mouth go dry before he draped the coat over the sofa's arm.

Where her mother or one of the other staff would probably find it and have to pick it up tomorrow morning....

Tanya had no idea why that crossed her mind.

But it was fleeting because then Tate sat down, leaving only enough space between them to angle toward her and stretch his left arm along the sofa back, faintly brushing her bare shoulder. That brought out the goose bumps again and made her wish he would curve that arm around her instead and pull her close....

"I'm sorry about tonight," he said then, drawing her out of her mental wanderings.

"I don't know what there is to be sorry for."

"I know I was lousy company."

"You weren't *lousy* company. Just... Well, it didn't seem as if you were enjoying yourself," she answered.

"I was enjoying being with you. Just not there."

"At the country club? You didn't mind it when we had dinner there," she pointed out.

"It's these big splashy affairs. I haven't had a lot of patience for them since—" he cut himself off, then "—in a while."

"Since your friend Buzz's death?" she asked. She hadn't pushed him on this before because she'd known it would bring down his spirits. Tonight they were already down and she thought it might do him some good to talk about it.

But once she'd asked that question she held her breath, unsure what his reaction would be.

"Actually," he said without any anger or compunction that she could see, "after Buzz died I didn't go to anything like this. I wasn't into socializing. It's just been since I got back from the Middle East that I've been expected to do it all again. And I'm finding it grating."

"Why is that?"

"A lot of reasons, I guess."

"You miss your friend all the more in places where you would have ordinarily seen him? Like tonight?" she guessed.

"Sure, there's some of that."

He made it sound as if missing his friend was not the major component but since he seemed to be willing to talk about Buzz, Tanya opted for going in that direction.

"His death must have been awful for you."

"It was a nightmare all the way around," Tate confirmed.

He swallowed hard enough for his Adam's apple to bob and Tanya was sorry she hadn't accepted that drink he'd offered earlier. She thought if she had, he might have had one, too, and she thought he could use it now.

But when she asked if he wanted one, he still declined.

"I can't imagine what it must have been like to see someone who was as close to you as a brother hurt so badly," she said, because she didn't know what else to say and she *couldn't* imagine it.

"It was…something," he said as if it had been too horrible to put into words.

"What made you want to go from that to the place where it had happened to him?" she asked because she was baffled by it.

"My family made the same argument. And I'm not sure I can explain it any better now than I could to them then. The contact I had with Buzz while he was over there was through letters and emails, an occasional phone call. But in every one of them he said he was glad he'd gone. That he thought he was helping and that was important. After he died… I don't know, I just had this *drive* to contribute something—something more than money—to what had been worthwhile to him at the end of his life. He'd said a lot about how much need there was outside of the military for medical care. That most of the organizations that go in and give aid weren't doing it—either because it was too dangerous or because the countries those organizations came out of didn't agree with what was going on. And when he died I wanted to do what he'd felt needed doing."

"In honor of him," Tanya said, feeling tears flood her own eyes.

But he hadn't let any fall and she didn't either. Blinking them back, she said, "So you joined the International Medical Corps—where the money from tonight's silent auction will go."

"The IMC, right."

"And you spent a year in Baghdad?" Tanya asked because she didn't know if she had the details straight.

"Primarily Baghdad, yes."

"What was it like?"

"Nothing like tonight," he said with a hint of distaste echoing in his tone. "It was intense. Eye-opening. There's nothing here to compare it to, that's for sure."

He went on to describe working until he dropped day after day under less-than-ideal conditions. Seeing patients injured in bombings and in the destruction that came with war. Operating on small children who would suffer a lifetime of infirmity due to their injuries.

He told her about what he'd seen of the hardships there, of his own rudimentary living arrangements, of eating food that was hardly country-club fare.

"If you want a rude awakening, I recommend it," he concluded.

"Being a war correspondent isn't really what I aspire to," she said. "I think I'll stick to the problems at home and trying to do what I can here. But it's no wonder you came back affected by it all."

His tight smile this time was more knowing. "But not *affected* the way everyone seems to think," he said. "I'm not depressed. I'm not suffering post-traumatic stress disorder. But I am...different."

"You don't like parties anymore..." she said, attempting to inject some levity.

"It isn't that I don't like them. I'm just having some trouble...feeling as if I fit in the way I did before. Embracing the excess after being where I've been and seeing what I've seen. It wasn't that spending my life wrapped in cotton—as you so colorfully put it the other night—made experiencing what I experienced in Iraq more than I could handle. It's that now I can't just roll myself back up in the cotton and go blithely on."

"Ohhh…" Tanya said as she finally understood what was happening with him. "Iraq was for you what living with my grandparents was for me—it took you out of the comfort of the cocoon and put you face-to-face with the real side of things."

"Exactly."

"And now you work in the clinic for the underprivileged and don't just *stroll in, cut and stroll out,*" she said, repeating what he'd given as one of the reasons he'd chosen surgery as his specialty. "Now you get involved with your patients—I know you made sure the ones who needed more help on Monday got it whether from other organizations or even by taking money out of your own pocket. You're hands-on."

He didn't seem to want his good deeds talked about because he shrugged all of that away and instead said, "Now I'm having trouble with all of this—" he motioned to the well-appointed room around them.

"Is that why you're staying in the guest-house?" she said as another light dawned for her.

"That's certainly part of it." He used an index finger to move her hair over her shoulder, brushing her bare skin in the process before he put his hand on the sofa back again.

"So how do you do it?" he asked then.

"How do I do what?"

"How do you go from reporting on people sleeping on the street to sleeping peacefully in your own warm, comfortable bed?"

"Is it guilt you're feeling?"

"Hey, you're the one who rubbed in the fact that I've led a pampered, useless life— are you going to tell me now that you don't think I *should* feel guilty?"

"Okay, I was basing that on the Tate I knew before. But that isn't who you are now," she said, meaning it because tonight he'd let her see just how true that was and why. "If you ask me, this Tate is a better one than the old, good-time-Charlie Tate. I believe you when you say you aren't depressed or suffering PTSD. I think you've just grown up. Matured. Developed a third dimension. Only now you have to learn to strike a balance—a middle ground between constant good-time-Charlie and the guy who has so much conscience—not guilt, conscience—that he can't go to a party and enjoy it. And yes, what I think is that guilt is the wrong label, I think it's *conscience*, and that developing a conscience that might not have been too evolved before is a good thing."

"And how do *you* strike that balance?" he challenged.

"When you went to the Middle East you didn't think you'd stop the war or be able to bring back your friend, did you?" she asked him rather than answering his question directly.

"Of course not."

"You just wanted to do what you could, right?"

"Right."

"And that's something. Even a drop in the bucket is still a drop. That's how I see it. You do what you can for others, then you take comfort where you can for yourself. It's like money in the bank—you spend some, you put some back. You can't feel guilty for replenishing, replenishing is what allows you to go on giving. If you *only* spend, after a while you're spent and you can't do any good at all because you don't have anything left to give. It's just that *your* replenishment is more lavish than most."

That made him laugh slightly, the way she'd hoped it would to ease a bit of the tension.

"In other words, I should just shut up and accept what I have?" he joked in return.

"As long as that isn't *all* you do—the way I think it was for you before. But from what I've seen of you this week, that *isn't* all you do now. I just don't think that means you can't go to a fancy country-club party or live in this house. Appreciate what you have. Share and do what you can. Balance."

"I appreciate you in that dress," he said, dropping his glance downward for a split second.

Did his change of subject mean he didn't want to talk about the more serious things anymore or that his spirits had lifted?

Tanya wasn't sensing the low spirits so much in him now but she didn't want to take credit for that, so she told herself Tate was just ready to talk about something else.

Which he continued to do when he said, "Did I tell you how fantastic you look?"

"I believe there was a *wow* involved."

"Looking at you, being there with you tonight was the only thing that got me through it. Thanks for coming with me."

"It was nice," she said, because while it might not have been perfect, it *had* been nice enough.

"Say you'll come to the Labor Day party on Monday night, too, so I can start appreciating that."

Tanya laughed. "I don't know...."

"All you *need* to know is that I want you there," he said.

His eyes were searching her face the way an art lover might look at a portrait—studying it as intently as if he were memorizing it. Things had changed in the atmosphere around them—calmed, quieted, turned somehow sensual—and that was so much better than before that Tanya just breathed a silent sigh of relief.

"Sometimes it seems like you're the older and wiser of the two of us," Tate said then, with an engaging smile.

"Oh, that's always what a girl wants to hear," Tanya joked, getting lost in the heat of that sky-blue gaze, in staring back into the face she couldn't seem to get enough of.

He grinned and slid his hand from the sofa back to mold his palm to the side of her neck. His fingertips were at her nape, his thumb was just behind her jaw and there was a nearly infinitesimal urging for her to tip her head up to him.

Tanya didn't resist, making it easy for him to lean forward and find her lips with his.

And that kiss was where the pattern of not-quite perfects ended, because it *was* perfect. So perfect that the moment it began, everything else seemed to fall away and leave nothing but the two of them.

How they'd achieved that kind of harmony so soon, Tanya couldn't fathom, but his mouth on hers felt absolutely natural, and she thought what she'd thought when he'd held her hand earlier—that it was as if they'd been doing it forever.

Lips parted in unison, breaths mingled and when his tongue came to hers it was like a secret only they could share.

Tate's right arm slipped under her thighs, bringing them over his so they could be closer still. Then that arm went around her, holding her while tongues cavorted, claiming each other with abandon.

Tanya's hands went to Tate's chest—a solid wall of steel that was nothing like her own breasts burgeoning from the tight, strapless dress and yearning for his touch.

No, no, no—that couldn't happen, she told herself. She wouldn't go that far.

But the craving was stubborn and stayed. Grew, in fact, as both his hands coursed around to the exposed flesh of her back and inspired more goose bumps.

Big, warm, adept hands that she knew would work magic on her far more sensitive front if only that was where they were....

Their kiss was deepening, mouths were open even wider, tongues were engaged in a sexy skirmish, things were awakening in Tanya that were wiping away rational thought and replacing it with pure, raw desire.

She felt her nipples harden and strain against the near prison they were bound in, and as she ran her hands around to Tate's back and pressed her fingers into the expanse of muscle there she wondered if she took a deep enough breath and arched her spine a little, if her breasts might just escape on their own....

But it didn't take anything quite that outrageous to draw Tate's attention in that direction as one of his hands began a slow path from her back to her side, and then to her breast. Cupping it, molding his palm around it the way he'd molded it to her neck before, he kneaded and caressed, pushed and pulled and tormented her by making her just want more.

But popping out of her dress apparently wouldn't have been as easy as a deep breath and an arch because Tate's hold was firm and even when he lifted more than she could have, the dress held tight.

Damn designer dress!

And oh, how she was dying to feel his touch on her bare breast!

She pulsed into his massaging hand, sighing softly when he let a single fingertip trail along the bodice's edge to tantalize the naked flesh above it.

But still she wanted more. Especially when she felt him harden at her thigh...

His mouth abandoned hers, kissing the hollow of her throat, the center of her breastbone, reaching the swell of one breast with the tip of his tongue as he hooked a finger between her cleavage and the dress and tried to make some headway like that.

Her nipples were both hard little gems of need but the dress offered no leeway and after a few attempts, Tate gave up on that route and reached for the zipper that ran from under her arm to her hip.

He discovered the hook that was at the top of it and unfastened that without too much trouble.

And Tanya thought, what would happen if she just gave in to this...

The dress would come off. Here in the den of the McCord mansion. His family's home. The house where she had rarely been allowed past the kitchen. The house her mother had spent years and years cleaning....

Tate eased the zipper down a scant inch.

And Tanya thought, what about the morning? Would one of the staff come in and find some tiny remnant that would give her away? Even just a bright red string from this dress she was itching to get out of now. Then everyone would know that she'd been in the house, with Tate....

Tate eased the zipper down another inch and by then she really could have freed herself from the boned bodice with only a deep breath.

But instead she thought again what she'd thought at saner moments than this, what if she *was* only a distraction for Tate tonight, an escape from his dark mood....

And then it was as if there were two of her. While half of her was still in his arms, wanting every bit of what he was clearly going to do, there was another part of her that was pulling away from his kiss, dragging her hands from his back and stopping him from unzipping that zipper any more.

"No, I can't. Not here or now or... I can't."

"We can go out to the guesthouse," he suggested, kissing her neck.

And it felt so good....

But she shook her head. "No. Not only not here. Not now—"

"Why not now?"

"It hasn't been a good night for you. I don't want to be...a diversion." Not from his feelings about losing his friend, not from his adjusting to his new vision of life, not from Katie Whitcomb-Salgar, who he could well end up with after all....

He sat up straight and looked at Tanya. "You are very diverting, though. How could you be anything else looking like that?" he said with a smile that spread languidly across his handsome face.

But she wouldn't allow herself to be *only* that and tonight she was too worried that that might be the case. So she again shook her head and merely repeated, "No."

He kissed her once more—softly, sweetly, enticingly, weakening her willpower and making it all the more difficult for her to stick with her decision.

Before she caved, though, he ended that kiss and she tried to strengthen her resolve by rezipping her dress.

Then Tate gallantly replaced her feet on the floor and stood, taking her hand and tugging her to stand.

"Come on, I'll walk you home," he said, continuing to hold her hand.

Tanya had just stepped away from the sofa when she remembered her evening bag.

"Wait," she said, reaching for it where it was being almost swallowed by the couch cushion, where her mother or one of the maids or Edward might have found it and begun to wonder....

Relieved that that possibility had been avoided, she told herself it was better that she hadn't let anything else happen to put her at risk.

If only her body agreed....

Tate led her through the house and out one of the rear doors. Neither of them said anything as they went to the housekeeper's cottage, and Tanya tried to be content with having her hand nestled in his for the trip.

Then they reached the bungalow and under the porch light Tate faced her again, laying a gentle palm on her cheek and looking deeply into her eyes.

"I'll do whatever you want. Or I won't do whatever it is you don't want me to do," he said in a deep voice that was for her ears alone. "But *I* want one thing clear—you aren't just a diversion to me. You're much, much more. So much more that I'm not even sure what, exactly. Something unlike what anyone else has ever been to me. Something special, I know that...."

He kissed her once more, softly, lingering, making her light-headed with wanting him all over again.

Then his hand slid from her face, his other hand let go of hers and he turned and walked away.

It took Tanya a very long while to recall

why it was that she'd stopped what she'd stopped in the den.

And even after she'd recalled it, there was still that part of her that wished she hadn't stopped it at all.

That part of her that just wanted to be anywhere, at anytime, if she could be with him....

Chapter Eleven

Katie Whitcomb-Salgar was back.

Actually, when JoBeth had told Tanya that, JoBeth had called her young Miss Whitcomb-Salgar because that was how JoBeth referred to the daughter of the McCords' friends. But in Tanya's mind—as it repeated itself over and over again to torture her—Tanya kept thinking *Katie Whitcomb-Salgar is back....*

And it *had* repeated itself over and over, and tortured her. All day and all evening, and it was keeping her from going to bed as midnight on Saturday night approached.

Of course it didn't help that her mother

had relayed the information at breakfast and that even though Tanya had gone looking for Tate repeatedly throughout the day and evening, he was nowhere to be found.

No, he and Tanya hadn't prearranged any time together today or tonight, and possibly he hadn't brought it up because he'd had other plans. Ordinary, everyday, innocent, other plans. But what if those other plans hadn't been so innocent? What if those other plans had been to see his longtime girlfriend on her first day home—that's what had troubled Tanya. What was still troubling her. What if he was off rekindling his romance with the heiress his family had handpicked for him?

Not that I should care, Tanya told herself.

But she *did* care. Too much to sleep, and so she decided that maybe a walk in the fresh night air might help. That maybe all the thoughts of Tate and all the thoughts of Tate reconciling with Katie Whitcomb-Salgar would just drift away....

Tanya made sure to leave the bungalow silently so she didn't wake her mother. Once she was outside she knew she should take her walk *away* from the McCord mansion, especially if she had any hope of walk-ing off thoughts of Tate. But at dinner her mother had talked about the fact that the lights for the Labor Day party were all up and how the lighting people had outdone themselves. Tanya could tell by the glow coming through the trees and shrubbery that the lights were lit. And she wanted to see them. *That* was why she went in that direction, she told herself, to see the lights. Not to see if Tate had ever come home.

Because it's none of my business...

Even if things had been heating up between them.

Even if he had said what he'd said the night before about her being more than a diversion to him. About her being special.

He could have just been trying to get her out of that dress she'd already taken to the dry cleaners so she could return it to him the way she'd told her mother she would.

As she stepped through the clearing into the backyard of the mansion it *was* the lights she was looking at. Hundreds and hundreds of tiny white lights wrapped all the tree trunks and lower branches and then canopied from there to the house itself. They spiraled up the poles that held the white tents where food and beverages would be served, they outlined the entire rear of the house and adorned the covered patio to cast a beautiful bright glow on the entire area.

It was only after a moment of enjoying the spectacle that Tanya realized there was someone gliding soundlessly through the pool water, doing laps.

It could have been Blake—he and Tate were about the same height, they had similar body types and coloring, and the swimmer's face was in the water so that even when he raised it to take a breath he was swimming away from her and she couldn't see it. But despite not having a clear view, it took only a moment for her to be sure it wasn't Tate's older brother. That it was Tate. And that he was alone.

Of course that didn't mean that he hadn't just come from hours and hours with Katie Whitcomb-Salgar, and Tanya knew she should turn and duck into the camouflage of the bushes once more before Tate saw her. That she should distance herself from him before he did get together with the other woman yet again, even if that hadn't already happened.

But there he was, moving through the water by the power of his long, muscular arms, his shoulder blades glistening in the light, flexing with each stroke, and she was riveted to that spot, watching him, appreciating the view....

He reached the opposite end of the Olympic-size pool, disappeared under the water for a minute and then resurfaced for the return lap.

It was definitely Tate—now he was coming in her direction, and each time his face turned out of the drink Tanya could see it in all its chiseled glory. But he wasn't yet aware of her, so she could still sneak away.

But she didn't. She just had to know if he'd been with Katie Whitcomb-Salgar today....

Tanya took a few more steps toward the pool and by the time Tate reached the end nearest to her, something—her movement probably—had caught his attention. He stopped rather than making a blind turn the way he had at the other end, and stood so that his shoulders rose out of the chest-high water. He ran his massive surgeon's hands up his face and into his hair to slick it back. Then he opened eyes that were the same color as the pool tiles and took in the sight of Tanya.

He smiled.

"Hi," he greeted simply.

"Hi," Tanya responded, sticking with simple even though there was nothing simple about what she was thinking and feeling at that moment.

"How about a swim?" he invited, spreading his arms wide and fanning his hands through the shimmering liquid around him.

"My suit's packed in a storage box somewhere," she said by way of declining.

His smile grew and one eyebrow arched devilishly as his gaze dropped to the tight tank top and blousy elastic-waisted short shorts she had on. "How about a clothes-optional swim?"

"I don't think so," Tanya said, hoping that he hadn't come from the other woman only to flirt with her the way he had been most of the last week. Worse than being a diversion to fill his time until he patched things up with his fiancée would be to be juggled along with Katie Whitcomb-Salgar....

"I just heard on the car radio that it's still ninety-two degrees. The water feels good," he persisted.

"Where were you coming from?" Tanya asked before she realized she was going to, wishing she'd managed more subtlety.

"The hospital. I got called in to do an

emergency surgery this morning. I've been in the O.R. for the last sixteen hours."

Not with Katie Whitcomb-Salgar....

Tanya couldn't help smiling. Grinning from ear to ear as relief washed over her and left her in an entirely different mood than she'd been in.

"What about you?" Tate asked. "I was going to whisk you away to take a look at some of the Foley oil wells for your report but since I didn't get to do that, what were you up to today?"

So it was her he'd planned to see today, even if he hadn't told her ahead of time....

Tanya went the rest of the way to the pool-side, sat down on the edge and dangled her feet in the water, knowing she shouldn't feel as good as she did, that the very fact that she did was an indication of just how hard it would have hit her if Tate *had* been with the other woman during the last several hours. But she felt so good she just had to go with it.

"I worked," she answered his question about how she'd spent the day. "I organized my notes and did some research on the Internet—apparently the Foleys were destined to be on the docket today no matter what because it was Foley research I did."

"Did you find out anything interesting?"

"To me, because I didn't really know much about them. I don't know if it's interesting to you. All I learned was that Rex Foley is the patriarch of the family and he recently left Foley Industries to start a consultancy. He has three kids. Zane, who *now* heads Foley Industries, Jason, who is the chief operating officer and a ladies' man—so no wonder you're worried about his involvement with Penny—and Travis, who's the rancher in the family. There's also one grandchild—Olivia—who is Zane's six-year-old daughter by his late wife," Tanya recited.

"Nothing new there for me," Tate decreed. And he didn't seem inclined to talk about his family's archenemies because then he said, "What about your evening? You didn't work tonight, too, did you?"

"Oh, tonight I had a hot date."

She'd only been joking but his frown said that wasn't how he'd taken it.

"Really? With an old boyfriend? Someone you knew before you moved away? Someone new?"

He was grilling her as if it was something he needed to know. Was that because he didn't like the idea of her being with someone else any more than she'd liked the possibility that he might have been with his former fiancée?

The mere chance that that was the case made Tanya feel better and better. She had to suppress a smile as she considered torturing him a little by drawing the joke out, but then she decided against it.

"I was kidding," she said. "I haven't met anyone since I've been back and as for someone from my past, I don't think Kevin—my high school sweetheart—would be interested in rekindling anything even if he *was* in Dallas—which he isn't."

Tate's smile made a reappearance. "That's it? *One* high school sweetheart? That's all you had?" he teased.

"Kevin Narcy," Tanya confirmed. "We went steady from ninth grade through graduation."

"Sounds serious."

"It was. As high school romances go. Just not serious enough to change either of our plans for after high school—Kevin dreamed of moving to Alaska and living some rustic, he-man lumberjack kind of life. I had no intention of doing *that*."

"Understandably. Did you part friends, and did he move to Alaska?"

"Yes on both counts—we parted friends and I wished him well when he climbed on the bus north. We even kept in contact for a while—as much as we could with him living in a cabin somewhere in the middle of nowhere, doing maintenance on the oil pipeline. But then he met a girl up there and got involved with her. I was invited to their wedding two years ago but I couldn't swing it, and since then I've just had Christmas cards."

"*He* got involved with someone else but you didn't?" Tate asked, obviously interested in her romantic history.

"Of course I did, too."

"Just one guy all the way through college?"

Tanya put her fingertips in the water and flicked a little at him because he made her sound so boring. "No, not *just one guy all the way through college,*" she repeated. "Although there was only one *serious guy*—I started going out with him my junior year and it lasted until about eight months ago."

"How serious?"

"Serious enough to talk marriage."

"That's all? You just talked about it?" Tate asked.

"And talked and talked and talked…"

"Why so much talk and no action?"

"Jordan just couldn't make up his mind— he kept going back and forth, back and forth. It seems like that's something you might be familiar with," Tanya goaded him.

"I don't know what you're talking about. I've never had any problem making up my mind—it's just that sometimes, when it's been about Katie, it might have *seemed* as if I made it up one way, then made it up another way, then made it up back to the first way again," he joked with some self-deprecation.

"Umm-hmm. Well, Jordan couldn't make up his mind about anything," Tanya continued. "He would order two full meals at dinner because he couldn't decide between them, and then have to eat part of my food, too, because it would look better to him and he'd think he should have ordered that instead. He is four years older than I am and had been in college long enough to have a degree by the time I started, but even after I'd finished my degree, he still didn't have one—"

"Not too smart?"

"It wasn't that. In fact, he had a nearly four-point grade average. He *could* have done anything he wanted. The problem was that he changed his major and what he wanted to be almost every semester. And when he did that, most of the credits he'd accumulated wouldn't count toward the new degree and he'd basically have to start over. He's up to his eyeballs in school loans and still hasn't graduated the last I heard. He can't vote because he can't settle on a candidate or a side on any issue. And he certainly couldn't commit completely to me or marriage or having kids."

"What if you had made the decision that he was going to marry you and just told him that was the way it was—so it wasn't a choice he had to make?"

"Right—that's just how I want someone to be with me—because I order them to and don't give them a choice. No thanks," Tanya said facetiously. "I finally decided enough was enough, I was sick of his back-and-forth, and I broke up with him—again, something you might have experienced...."

"I have not experienced just two serious relationships in my life," he said with a sly half smile that let her know he was purposely misunderstanding her.

"No, *you've* only had *one* serious relationship. That's on and off and on and off and on and off...."

"I beg your pardon. I've had several serious relationships."

Tanya rolled her eyes. "Who besides young Miss Whitcomb-Salgar?" she challenged in disbelief.

"There was Heather McGinnley," he said with an exaggeratedly rapturous expression and tone. "She was my seventeen-year-old camp counselor when I was fifteen. I gave her my virginity and a marriage proposal."

Tanya laughed. "Wow, you were really grateful."

"Hey!" Tate chastised, laughing too. "It wasn't gratitude, it was love."

"But then you came home from camp and—"

"Yes, then I came home from camp and there was Katie," he acknowledged, "and I had to honor my obligation to escort her to Junior Cotillion. But Heather had turned me down, anyway, so what's a guy to do? But that doesn't mean I was any less *seriously* head over heels with Heather before she rejected me."

"So, two serious relationships—sort of," Tanya allowed. "That's the same as me."

"Then there was Marnie Wilson, the life-guard at the country-club pool," Tate added. "We had three very serious summers together and might have had more than the summers except that she spent the rest of the time away at boarding school."

"And in between there was—"

"Yes, Katie," he granted. "But I was still serious about Marnie when I was with her."

"And even though I'm sure you can go on with a half-dozen more brief—but serious—interludes that you had through college and medical school, the bottom line is that the only *genuinely* serious relationship you've had was with Katie Whitcomb-Salgar."

"You can just call her Katie—I'll know who you're talking about. And you're wrong again. Yes, there have been a lot of on-and-offs with Katie and me but that doesn't mean I wasn't *serious* about anyone in between. The other relationships just didn't pan out. But if they had… Who knows?" he concluded.

"I know I'm sticking with you just having *one* serious relationship," Tanya persisted.

"And I could argue that the relationship with Katie didn't have all the earmarks of a serious relationship itself."

"*That* seems like a stretch."

"Not really," Tate said as he hoisted himself out of the water and sat on the pool's edge beside her.

Tanya's pulse sped up a notch at the sight of him in nothing but trunks, his massively muscled thighs dwarfing hers there on the deck, so much of him bare....

"The *real* bottom line with Katie and me," he was saying, forcing Tanya to concentrate on the subject and not on his magnificent body, "is that we weren't serious enough about our relationship. At least I wasn't. Which is why there were so many breaks from it, why it was so easy for us to *be* on-again, off-again. And, ultimately, that's why we ended it for good this time. I told you, we finally admitted to ourselves that we're more friends than anything else. That it was family pressure—not fate or destiny or any really strong feelings—putting us together."

"Maybe it's fate that keeps urging your families to pressure you and Katie to be together," Tanya suggested, testing him.

"Or maybe it was fate that put you behind the library desk last week...."

"I hate to tell you, but it was families—not fate—that put us together, too," Tanya said, her voice quiet even though she was trying not to let him or his words or the look of appreciation in those eyes get to her. "Remember that you and I only know each other because your mother hired my mother."

Tate grinned. "I didn't think of that. But it doesn't change my mind—I still believe it was fate that brought you back here, now, just when I needed a little color and life and energy injected into things."

"I'm a shot in the arm?" she joked.

"A shot in the arm that I must need because I was hating the thought that today was going to go by without my getting to see you. And then I opened my eyes a few minutes ago and there you were and…" He shook his head as if in awe. "It was definitely a pick-me-up." He suddenly grinned a wicked grin and added, "In more ways than one…"

This time it was Tanya who chose to misconstrue what he was implying. "I'm just glad that you're happier than you were last night."

He bent over and kissed the top of her shoulder, sending little shards of glitter sparkling along her nerve endings.

"Oh, I'm happy all right," he assured her.

"And not because Katie is back in Dallas?" Tanya said, testing still.

Tate leaned farther over and kissed her just behind the shoulder. "I didn't know she was," he said without any indication that he cared.

"That's what I heard," Tanya persisted.

"Okay."

He kissed the top of her shoulder a second time and then the front of it and Tanya wished it didn't feel like heaven. It was just so difficult to deny herself when everything he did made her want him all the more.

"She's always going to be a part of your circle.... Katie is...isn't she?" Tanya felt compelled to say for her own sake, reminding herself.

"It doesn't matter," he assured her in a voice growing more husky by the minute.

Then he slipped into the water again, standing directly in front of her. His hands came around her calves and he pulled her in with him before she even realized what he was doing.

The surprise of it and that initial jolt of cold made her gasp, and she had the impression that a shock was what he wanted to cause.

"I respect Katie. I like her. I care about her as a friend. But as far as anything else goes, she and I are done. So no more Katie," he decreed. "No more Katie in any important way in my life, and definitely not in tonight or anything that has to do with you and me. Got it?"

He was staring down at Tanya intently and with so much heat in his eyes that it was almost enough to wipe away the coolness that she was submerged in to her neck. But still she raised a saucy chin to him and said, "You're laying down the law?"

He smiled and his hands went to her upper arms, clasping them in a firm grip. "That's only the start of what I want to lay down," he said under his breath before he caught her mouth with his in a way that was as if no time had passed between last night and this, as if everything that had ignited in the den then had just simmered below the surface in him until that moment, and at that moment it had bubbled up, demanding to have its day.

Not only in Tate, though. In Tanya, too, she realized as her answer to his kiss was every bit as hungry as his, as her hands went to those amazing pectorals she'd been dying to know the feel of. Her own nipples—already perked up by the cold—now hardened into tiny pebbles instantly striving for his touch.

She struggled against her own inclinations to recall *why* she hadn't let this happen last night.

They'd been in the main house, the McCord house. Tate had had a bad night that had brought up his feelings about his friend's death and she hadn't wanted to just be a diversion from that. Or a diversion he filled the time with when he *was* off-again with Katie.

But tonight...

They weren't exactly *in* the McCords' house and could easily sneak away to the guest cottage nearby.

He wasn't looking for a quick fix for bad feelings about losing his friend.

But could she believe that he was genuinely finished with Katie Whitcomb-Salgar and not only in an intermission?

Maybe she was fooling herself but she had the sense that *Tate* believed it. And if he believed it, didn't that strengthen the possibility that things between Katie and him really, truly, once and for all, were over?

Or do I just want him so much I'm talking myself into it?

Because as mouths opened wide and Tate's tongue came to claim hers and teach it a tango all their own, she *did* want him so much it hurt....

His hands went from her arms to her breasts and the thin, wet layers of her tank top and built-in bra were nothing like the armor that the designer dress had been. It wasn't exactly like having her skin enveloped in his, but it was still good enough to make her nipples strain into his palms as if they only existed for that.

He has to be through with the other woman, she thought. *He just has to be.*

Because tonight, no matter what, Tanya didn't have the strength to say no....

She ran her hands all over him—from the tautness of his lower back up the widening vee to broad shoulders, down impressive biceps, across to a chest where his own nipples were mimicking hers.

And all the while that kiss!

It was open and urgent and enough to drive her out of her mind all on its own....

Maybe it also let Tate know just how willing she was tonight because he took his hands from her breasts, scooped her into his arms and carried her up the pool steps and out of the water. He had to stop kissing her to watch where he was going but even so he didn't ask permission, he merely took her to the guesthouse.

To the guesthouse's bedroom...

Of course Tanya could have objected. But she didn't.

Once they were secluded in his room and she was on her own two feet again, Tate didn't hesitate to peel off her wet tank top and warm her breasts with his hands first, and then with his mouth. After a moment, he took off her shorts and his swimsuit in quick succession.

Then there they were, and for a brief moment it was almost inconceivable to Tanya that she was actually standing there naked, facing an also naked Tate McCord. But the unreality of it passed almost instantly as wanting him overwhelmed the awkwardness. And from that moment on nothing seemed anything but right.

Tate again whisked her into his arms and laid her on the bed. The curtains were open and moonlight cast a spotlight's glow on him as he stood at the bedside, savoring the sight of her.

She did the same, feasting on the magnificence of a body no sculptor would ignore as that milky light caressed him the way Tanya's hands ached to. And did the moment he joined her, stretching out next to her, lying on his side, his front running the length of her as his mouth rediscovered hers and one of his hands closed around her bare breast once more.

Massaging, kneading, gently plucking at her nipple with agile, talented fingers while mouths again did a sexy reunion kiss that took no time to turn into a randy, uninhibited plundering.

But even a surgeon's hands could only perform so much and Tanya had no complaints when his mouth abandoned hers a second time to kiss a trail from there to the hollow of her throat, to her collarbone, to her breast....

Tiny, feathery kisses were what he placed all around first one nipple and then the other, teasing her, tantalizing her with anticipation before his lips parted enough to draw her between them, and then—at last—to pull her whole breast into the divine warmth of his open mouth.

Tanya's spine arched off the mattress in response to the delights he was unveiling, to flicks of his tongue and tender tugs of his teeth, to his other hand at her other breast, kneading and pressing and—rather than satisfying her—only making her want even more.

She sent her own hands exploring then, boldly, brazenly, coursing all over him again until she found the long, steely shaft that announced how much he wanted her, too.

A low moan of pleasure rumbled from his throat as he draped a heavy thigh over hers. And while his mouth continued its wonders at her breast, the hand that was titillating the other slid away.

With his palm flat against her, that hand traveled down to her stomach, down farther to the juncture of her legs, following the curve of her body to dip between them. And just when Tanya thought she'd been driving him a little crazier than he'd been driving her, he proved her wrong.

Long fingers worked a magic of their own, inside of her and out, raising new levels of need that she hadn't even known she was capable of, leaving her right on the brink.

As if he knew that, he rose above her,

recapturing her mouth with his as he positioned himself between her thighs, probing with that portion of him she'd just released. Finding his home, he slipped into her slowly, smoothly, sleekly, until he was embedded deeply within her.

He pulsed there several times. Then he stopped kissing her and dipped to her breast again, sending only the tip of his tongue to the very crest of her breast as his hips began to move—barely in and out in the same slow, measured rhythm his tongue was keeping at her nipple.

But that didn't last for long before his hips picked up speed and force, before his back arched so he could plunge into her, before he devoted himself to those fabulous thrusts that fitted them together flawlessly.

Tanya kept pace, meeting him, matching him, holding tight for the ride that took them up another notch each time he came into her, each time he drew out. Passion, need grew. Bigger and bigger, like a giant balloon carrying her higher and higher until Tanya reached the pinnacle and couldn't do anything but cling to Tate while crystal clear, pristine pleasure held her at the very peak for one mindless moment. One moment when Tate, too, reached the same climax, buried so deeply within her that they were nearly melded together.

And then it began to ebb, to deflate and, in perfect sync, they both slowly drifted back from that shared bliss.

Muscles relaxed and Tate let more of his weight rest on her, his cheek pressed to hers, his breath a hot breeze on her shoulder.

But it was only a few minutes before his arms insinuated themselves around her so he could roll them to their sides, bodies still joined and molded together into one.

Then his lips were on the top of her head, in her hair, placing a reverent kiss there before he whispered, "What you do to me is like nothing I've ever known."

There was a sort of reverence in his tone, too, and all Tanya could do was kiss the marvelous chest she was facing and whisper in return, "Me, too."

That was how they stayed until she felt him beginning to fall asleep. Then he caught himself, finally slipped out of her and laid on his back, pulling her as close as he could to lie alongside him with her head cradled on his shoulder.

His arms around her were still tight

enough to let her know he wasn't letting her go. And while she hated the thought of her mother or any other member of the staff finding out about this, she couldn't make herself roll away from him and leave.

As if he knew that was what she was thinking, Tate said, "Don't go anywhere. I just need a catnap. But I don't want this to end…."

She assumed he meant that he didn't want tonight to end yet, and since she didn't either, she merely said, "Okay."

But as she drifted into sleep, too, it did fleetingly cross her mind that he might have been referring to something more than tonight when he'd said he didn't want this to end.

She was too tired and replete herself, though, to explore it, and so she just let herself drift closer to sleep in Tate's arms, feeling more at home there than she'd ever felt anywhere.

And just this once, letting that be all that mattered.

Chapter Twelve

It was four-thirty Sunday morning and Tate was standing in the doorway of the guesthouse watching Tanya leave. They'd bounced from making love to sleeping to making love to sleeping all night, but even though he'd done his damnedest to persuade her to stay longer, she wouldn't. Not and risk that any of the staff—especially her mother—might be starting work early and discover that she'd spent the night with him. She wouldn't even let him walk her home. She'd said that if she was alone and got caught she could say she'd just gone out for an early morning jog.

But Tate had never been so sorry to see anyone go.

As he stood there enjoying the view of her compact rear end in those short shorts, of her silky hair falling around her shoulders, hating it when she disappeared down the path to the housekeeper's cottage, he was also thinking about what he'd said in response to her notion that she was only some kind of distraction for him. He was thinking about the fact that even then he'd told her that she was more than that.

He hadn't been able to define exactly *what,* but now it struck him.

It had already occurred to him that, with Tanya, he felt some of the same kinship he'd felt with Buzz, the same freedom to open up and be himself. After talking to her *about* Buzz, about this last year and a half, he knew more than ever just how true that was.

And when he'd confided in Tanya, she'd altered his view of things. She'd been instrumental in putting so many things that had been bothering him—weighing on him—into focus.

Conscience, not guilt. Replenishing. Striking a balance—those were all things that Tanya had steered him in the direction of.

And the more he'd thought about it since she'd said it, the more he'd realized that she was right.

Which meant that she had an insight that not even Buzz had had.

She was insightful, bright, smart....

Not that Katie wasn't intelligent, too—she was. And just as caring and considerate and compassionate as Tanya. But where Tanya was different from Katie was in Tanya's willingness to use her intelligence to go head-to-head with him. Katie *could* have, but in their relationship, with Katie's nature, she just wouldn't do or say anything that might have stepped on his toes or ruffled his feathers. She would have appeased, not challenged.

Tanya, on the other hand, had no compunction about challenging him. Challenging his opinions, his views. Boldly, bravely, without any signs that she cared who he was or what he might think.

And he'd liked that. He'd gotten a kick out of it.

And out of just about everything else he'd done with her.

Oh, yeah, he had fun with her, there was no doubt about that. She was a breath of fresh air. Her energy, her enthusiasm, were infectious. There was just never a moment when he'd been bored or wished he was anywhere else, with anyone else.

And that was all on top of the fact that she was beautiful and sexy. That he could look at that exquisite face until his eyes ached and still not have his fill. That his hands itched to be all over her all the time. That his own body was hard to control the minute she got anywhere around him.

And after these last hours together? He'd meant it when he'd told her that what she did for him in bed was like nothing he'd ever known before.

Maybe, he thought as he continued to look down the path she'd followed, Tanya wasn't merely a lot of things to him.

Maybe she was everything to him....

That was kind of a crazy thought.

And yet, the longer he rolled it around in his head, the less crazy it began to seem.

When he thought about talking through problems, through issues and difficulties, there wasn't anyone he wanted to talk to more than Tanya.

When he thought about going anywhere in the world, at anytime, to anyplace, there wasn't anyone he wanted to be with more than Tanya.

When he thought about sharing the best—and the worst—life had to offer, there wasn't anyone he wanted to share any of it with more than Tanya. There wasn't anyone he knew who he *could* share even the worst with the way he knew he could share it with her.

And when he thought about how much he'd just plain wanted her almost since the minute he'd seen her, about holding her, kissing her, making love to her? There wasn't anyone else.

And more than that, he suddenly knew there never could be.

None of that was anything he'd ever thought about Katie. Not that he would want Katie to know that and hurt her, but it was true. Somehow, from out of nowhere, he'd suddenly found the one person who was everything to him. And it wasn't Katie. It never had been. It was Tanya.

She'd said that he'd finally developed a third dimension, that he'd grown up, matured. And maybe he had. But the truth for him was that *she* was what made him feel complete and well-rounded and grounded and able to take whatever it was that had changed in him and use it to the best advantage. She was the reason he'd come to be comfortable with it.

The truth was that it was Tanya who replenished him. Who struck a balance for him. Who made everything worthwhile.

He'd just been settling before and he saw that now, too. He'd told Tanya that Katie was great and that was true. But Katie had just never made him feel what Tanya made him feel.

And what he felt was a driving need to have Tanya in his life. Not just on the peripheries of it—center stage, starring role, main focus.

But she wouldn't even stay with him until the sun came up....

On the other hand, maybe if she—and everyone else—knew how much she mattered to him, how important she was to him, she wouldn't be so determined to hide what they had together.

He had to hope so.

Because now that he knew that she was the world to him, he couldn't imagine anything without her.

And as soon as that sun did rise and her mother left her alone, he was going to make sure she knew that....

* * *

After a night of more lovemaking than sleep, Tanya was snoozing pretty deeply at nine o'clock when a demanding knock on the cottage's front door woke her. And even after she was awake enough to get her bearings and realize what all the racket was, she waited a moment, hoping her mother hadn't left yet and would answer it so she could go back to sleep.

But the knocking kept up and she finally got out of bed.

She'd taken a quick shower when she'd returned from the guesthouse. After that she'd put on a pair of pajama pants and a T-shirt—both concealing enough to go to the door in. She wasn't expecting it to matter so she merely ran her fingers through her hair to push it away from her face and—makeupless—she opened the front door.

To find Tate—freshly showered and shaved, hair neat and clean, wearing jeans and a T-shirt that fit him like a second glorious skin.

"Ohhh, I'm not presentable," Tanya moaned when she glanced blearily into his clear, alert eyes.

Tate merely smiled as if he liked the bed-head look. "I had to see you. I was watching for your mother to go up to the house so I'd know when she was gone."

Tanya was at least grateful for that. Not that she wasn't glad to see him—she was *always* glad to see him. Elated, in fact. She just didn't like being at a disadvantage in the grooming department. And she was a little concerned that he thought they could have privacy here when she knew better.

"You can't…come in. Mama could come back anytime or someone could see you…."

"I want to talk. If your mother comes back and finds us doing that, so what?"

His expression was happy but there was something intense and insistent in his attitude that Tanya didn't quite understand. Still, she supposed if all they did was talk….

"I'm sure Mama left coffee. Why don't you pour two cups and take them out on the patio where we had lunch? I'll be right there," she said.

"Just hurry."

Tanya could hear him in the kitchen and then going out the French doors in back as she rushed through brushing her teeth and her hair, pinching her cheeks and applying a touch of mascara. She didn't waste time doing more than that, however, because she was too curious about what was going on with him. It didn't occur to her until she was on her way through the house to join him that maybe he'd had an early morning phone call from Katie. Or a visit. Or some contact that had rekindled things between them. And that now he'd made a beeline here to tell her....

That put a damper on things and by the time she sat across from him at the patio table she was feeling a whole lot more reserved.

"What's up?" she asked.

His smile made him look very pleased with himself. "A lot that I needed to talk to you about right away."

Because now that he'd made the conquest of the housekeeper's daughter he'd come to say it was Katie he should be with after all and he wanted Tanya to keep quiet?

That seemed too likely to Tanya and her stomach knotted. Which meant that even though she could have used a shot of caffeine, she ignored the coffee because she didn't think she could get it down. And she just kept thinking that the housekeeper's daughter might be who a McCord slept with, but a Katie Whitcomb-Salgar was who ultimately got the man himself....

"I'm listening," she said in response to his claim that he needed to talk.

Tate slid his chair around the table so he could be closer to her and then yanked her chair to face his, leaving them sitting knee to knee. Then he leaned his elbows on his thighs and took her hands in his.

To comfort her when he gave her the bad news? she wondered.

And yet his touch still felt so good, so familiar, it almost made her melt on the spot....

"You've done a lot to open my eyes since we've been hanging out," he said then. "But this morning when you left, they really opened—"

"Katie called," Tanya blurted out what she was so afraid he was going to say.

Tate smiled a confused smile followed quickly by a dazed frown. "No. Why would that have anything to do with...." Light dawned for him. "No, Katie didn't call and it wouldn't have mattered if she had. I told you Katie and I are through. What I realized this morning was that nothing I ever felt for her or had with her could compare to what I feel for you, what you and I have together."

"We don't really have anything together," Tanya pointed out quietly, still worried about where he was going with this.

"We have a lot together," he countered. "Maybe not friends or life experience or lifestyle or what it was that made it seem like Katie was right for me. But what you and I have is so much more. It's everything...."

He said that with a small chuckle, as if it had a meaning for him that she wasn't privy to.

Then he went on. "That's what came to me this morning—that you're everything to me. Sometimes being with you is like being with Buzz—freeing, calming, relaxing, just fun. Sometimes being with you gives me a break from everything—you're like a tropical vacation. Sometimes it forces me to be on my toes, to keep my debating skills up. It's always the way I think it *should* have been with Katie to ever have considered marrying her, only with you it's even better than I thought it could be—the physical, the emotional, all of it. It's always just great—there hasn't been a single minute of it that I've wanted to end. I hate it when it does, and I want it to start again as soon as I can make it. What all that boiled down to for me this morning is that I just don't want it to ever end. So here I am and I know this is quick and unexpected and maybe a little crazy, but I want you to be my—"

"I'm your housekeeper's daughter," Tanya cut him off, not letting him finish what it seemed he might have been about to say. What she would have liked to hear.

But what if she heard it? Nothing else would be changed, she'd still have to refuse him and she wasn't sure she'd be able to....

"It doesn't make any difference that you're the housekeeper's daughter," Tate persisted.

"Maybe not to you. It makes a lot of difference to me. And to my mother. And probably to your mother and the rest of your family and friends. Your mother, your family and friends not only wouldn't like you being with someone from the back side of the bushes, but they've already picked out who they *do* want you to be with."

"And I tried to go with that and it didn't work. For Katie or for me. What works for me is you."

Tanya shook her head. "You lost your friend. You spent time in a part of the world where awful things are happening. You're adjusting to a lot of changes in your life, in yourself, you've had problems getting back into the swing of things with the people who have always mattered to you. You just think—"

"It's not as if I'm delusional, Tanya. I've known what was going on with me all along but it took you to show me how to deal with it, to give me a new and better perspective. And you aren't only a diversion, either—if that's what you're getting at. Thinking that is selling yourself short."

"Okay, let's say that's true. It doesn't alter the fact that I am who I am, and you are who you are. I might as well be a Foley—I wouldn't be any more welcome or at home than they would."

"Even the Foleys have wiggled their way in here and there—with my mother and now with Penny."

"And you're none too happy about that!" Tanya pointed out.

She also thought about the charity dinner. Yes, his friends and family had been cordial, but none of them had known how to relate to her, how to make more than polite, surface conversation with her. They might as well have spoken different languages.

But more than his family, it was her own situation that held Tanya back. Especially when she thought about Edward the butler bringing her the dress when it was delivered from the designer, when she thought about him learning that Tate would be paying the bill. It had been so awkward. So embarrassing.

And she wasn't even as close to Edward as she was to some of the other staff. To her mother....

"My mother *works* for you."

"A lot of people work for us—"

"She's cleaned your house. *Served* you. She depends on you for the roof over her head."

"So if she was my secretary or my surgical assistant, that would be different?"

"I don't know," Tanya said because she didn't. What she did know was that growing up here had made her well aware that there was a distinct line between the people who served the McCords and the McCords themselves. Between the people who catered to their lives and the people the McCords socialized with and most certainly coupled with. And that she was on the side of the people who catered to them, not the side of the people they socialized and coupled with.

"All I can tell you," she continued, "is that I can't sit at your dining room table and be served by someone I was borrowing shampoo from last week. I can't be chauffeured by the man who used to fix my bicycle, who put bandages on my scraped shins, who taught me to drive. I can't sleep in a bed turned down by my mother's best friend or put my own mother to the tasks she does for your family. I wouldn't."

"So don't. All of that can be worked out. It isn't important—"

"That's right, it isn't important to you. Because what goes on with the staff beyond meeting your needs is their problem, their business. But it *is* my business and it *is* important to me—that's the point."

"But you're talking details that can be sorted out. I'm talking a much bigger picture. I'm talking about your future and mine, about us having a life together."

A complicated life—that's what her mother had said about the life he led. And how he might escape from it for a while with her, but that eventually he would go back to it. Which Tanya thought he could do at anytime now that he seemed on top of what had been bogging him down before. The problem was that he was trying to sign her on for the return trip, and she was too afraid that once he got back in the center of that circle, the fact that she didn't belong there would be their undoing.

And then what?

Her mother would likely be out of a job, for one thing.

But even worse than that, Tanya didn't think she could bear discovering that she honestly couldn't be a part of his world, that he might be ashamed of her, that she might embarrass him. That when the blush of his infatuation with her dimmed, he would take a look at her, a look at Katie Whitcomb-Salgar and realize he'd made a mistake....

"Yours isn't a life I want," she said, holding her chin as high as she could, making it sound as if she was firm in that decision.

"You don't want the life, or you don't want me? Because they're not the same thing."

"They are the same thing. It's *your* life. A life my mother was right to remove me from when I was a kid because it *isn't* my life. It can't be. And I don't want it to be." Not when she was so convinced that she would eventually come up short in it and lose him anyway. Lose him and her mother's livelihood and her own pride along with it all....

"There's just too much at stake, Tate," she said. "Last night was..." Why was her voice cracking? She wasn't going to cry! She wouldn't let herself.

She cleared her throat. "The last week, last night—it's all been amazing, I won't deny that. But in the cold light of day today, when you're talking about the *future?* You still belong on your side of the bushes and I still belong on this one."

"I'll cut the damn bushes down!"

"That's the point—even if you wanted to do that, no one else on either side would stand for it."

He shook his head firmly. "No, Tanya, I'm not taking that as an answer."

"It's my answer. You can't change it."

"But you can. You want to break down barriers for a living, expose wrongs, change things—start here."

"I don't think it would make any difference

here. I only think it would do damage." To her. To her mother. And she wouldn't do that.

"Tanya, I'm in love with you!"

Her breath caught in her lungs at those words that everything in her wanted to hear, wanted to be able to rejoice in.

But as heartfelt as they sounded, she still wasn't sure that whatever he was feeling was real or enduring or anything she should count on. She thought it was more of an exuberance he was experiencing as he emerged from the low point he'd been in. And that wouldn't last.

Tanya swallowed hard and forced herself to breathe again. But the best she could manage was a whispered, "I'm sorry," before she pulled her hands out of his.

"Don't do this," he said. "You're wrong and you're ruining so much for both of us."

But she only repeated, "I'm sorry."

Then she stood and went into the house because she knew she couldn't keep from crying for much longer and she wouldn't do that in front of him.

She made it as far as the laundry room and ducked in where she knew Tate couldn't see her before she crumpled against the dryer and sobbed.

And that was when she admitted to herself that while she might not believe that Tate genuinely loved her, she was very much afraid that she might have genuinely fallen in love with him....

Chapter Thirteen

"Tate McCord *proposed* to you?"

It was after four o'clock on Monday afternoon. In the midst of last-minute, hectic preparations for the McCords' Labor Day party, JoBeth had hustled into the cottage for a sandwich and, while she was throwing it together, had demanded to know what was going on with Tanya and Tate.

Because her mother was so busy with the party, Tanya had been able to keep a low profile since Tate's visit Sunday morning. *This* morning JoBeth had noticed her lethargy and swollen eyes, but Tanya had said it must be allergies. She'd known her mother was skeptical, but JoBeth hadn't had the time to explore it.

Then, apparently, during the course of the day, JoBeth had overheard the gardeners talking about seeing Tate storm away from the housekeeper's bungalow Sunday. Added to an unusually heated argument between Tate and his brother Blake over Katie Whitcomb-Salgar at lunchtime—during which Tate had apparently shouted that Katie Whitcomb-Salgar was the last thing on his mind—JoBeth had put two and two together. And come home to Tanya for the truth.

Knowing how relentless her mother could be, Tanya had given in without much resistance and told her mother the whole story.

"It wasn't a formal, will-you-marry-me proposal, no," Tanya answered her mother's shocked question. "But I think that was what he was saying, yes."

"And you said no?"

It hadn't occurred to Tanya until hours later on Sunday that Tate could fire her mother out of retribution, and with that on her mind now, too, she could only apologize to JoBeth the way she had to Tate yesterday morning. "Yes, I said no. And I'm sorry,

Mama. I don't think it will hurt your job but it's probably better if I get an apartment right away—out of sight, out of mind—just for safekeeping."

While she ate more of her sandwich, Jo-Beth waved that away, obviously unbothered by it. "It isn't as if I'd have you marry a man just to save my job, Tanya. But by the same token, I wouldn't have you *not* marry someone you want to marry because of it."

"I didn't say I wanted to marry him," Tanya said quietly.

"But you do. Look at you—this is not *allergies.* And I heard you up pacing most of the night."

"Everything with Tate just came out of the blue and surprised me," Tanya said. "Having something serious with him—a *future* with him—isn't something I'd ever thought about." Although she'd thought about almost nothing else since…

"But you do want to marry him," JoBeth repeated.

"It's complicated—maybe that's what happens when you let yourself get involved with someone who leads a complicated life," Tanya said, referring to her mother's past words.

"But you do want to marry Tate," JoBeth repeated yet again.

"I don't know, Mama!" Tanya snapped.

JoBeth let a moment of silence follow to relay her lack of appreciation for having her head bitten off. She didn't say anything about Tanya's outburst, though. Instead, after finishing half of her sandwich, she said, "My position here is not the reason for you to say no if you want to say yes. Either I'm hired help who makes the schedule and tells the staff what to do, or I'm the in-law on the payroll who makes the schedule and tells the staff what to do."

"You don't think it would be weird if you were the in-law who did it?"

"Weird becomes normal if you give it enough time. And I'd certainly have job security," JoBeth said.

"Unless of course I married him and six months down the road he realized that I don't belong with his family and friends, and Katie Whitcomb-Salgar looks good to him again—the way she always has before when one of their breakups ended."

"So my job isn't the only reason you said no."

"It was only one of them—a big one, but

only one. You've reminded me yourself that Tate and Katie always get back together. And of course I know how things are—a *McCord* isn't supposed to *marry* the help. And I'm happy with who I am, I like it, I *want* to be in touch with the real world the way you sent me to Grandma and Grandpa to be. I don't want to be a *McCord*."

"Another of the reasons I sent you to spend time with your grandparents was because I didn't want you to want what you couldn't have. But you want Tate. And wanting what you *can* have? I don't know that you should turn your nose up at that, Tanya."

"But like I said, even if I *can* have Tate now, will it last? And wouldn't it be so much worse to have him for a while and then lose him because one day he regrets that I'm *not* Katie Whitcomb-Salgar?"

"What does Tate have to say on the subject of young Miss Whitcomb-Salgar?"

Tanya told her mother all of Tate's claims that he and Katie were nothing but friends and never again would be engaged.

"And you don't believe him?" JoBeth asked.

"It isn't that. But you know how many times they've called it quits and then started up again. I'm sure he believed it was over every time. And it wasn't."

"But he's different now than he was before."

That was true and Tanya couldn't refute it. But did the change in him mean that the back-and-forth with Katie was over?

"He is different," Tanya conceded rather than address the issue of whether or not that was any guarantee that he was finished with the other woman. "But the rest of his family and friends aren't and they have their hearts set on him being with Katie. There's bound to be pressure for that and all the more disapproval of me because I'm standing in the way of that."

"But if it really is over between them Tate won't go back with her because other people want him to. So his family and friends will just have to be disappointed and learn to live with it. And if Tate honestly has changed and doesn't feel as if he completely fits in with everyone anymore, doesn't that clear the way for the two of you to carve out a place of your own that isn't altogether on his side of the fence—so to speak—or altogether on yours?"

"We'd be *in* the bushes?" Tanya muttered

to herself, knowing her mother wouldn't understand the reference to what she and Tate had talked about.

Then, to JoBeth she said, "I don't know. I suppose it's possible that we could make a niche of our own. But it still wouldn't take away the risk that eventually Tate might want to be back in the heart of his circle, and not with the housekeeper's daughter at his side."

"So I suppose what you can do is try to figure out if you think this change in Tate is permanent or temporary. And no matter what you think, decide if you want him enough to take the risk on him."

JoBeth glanced at the clock on the wall. "I shouldn't have been away this long on a party day. I have to get back," she announced as she set her dish and the other half of her sandwich in the sink.

But still she hesitated to leave Tanya, looking at her daughter with sympathetic eyes. "I hate to see you so mopey," she said. "And poor Tate, he seems just as miserable. I thought he was down before, but now? This is as bad as he was right after word came that his friend was hurt."

Tanya felt guilty for being comforted and

satisfied at hearing that Tate felt awful, too. But she did.

"I know he invited you tonight," JoBeth went on. "Maybe you should come."

"And help you tell the kitchen staff to wash glasses and serve dessert, or hide that you and I are mother and daughter when I'm introduced to the governor?"

"I'll take care of the glasses and the dessert and when I see you with the governor I'll come over and you can introduce me, too," JoBeth said, solving the problem simply. Then she gave Tanya a hug before she headed for the door to leave.

But before she did, she turned back to Tanya and added, "I always wanted you to have more in life than I did, Tanya. I wanted you to have your education, to have a career you chose—not just the best job you could get under the circumstances. You've done that and I'm proud of you. Proud of the person you are and proud of your accomplishments and successes. But most of all, I just want you to be happy. If Tate McCord makes you happy, then... Well, where there's a will, there's a way. That may not be something Tate had to learn, but it's something you did. And don't ever—*ever*—

let me be what blocks that way. Or any other people, either."

When her mother left the cottage Tanya sat at the kitchen table where her notes were spread out. She'd been trying all day long to get some work done on her report but today, like Saturday, cataloging information on the McCords didn't help keep her from thinking about Tate.

Plus the sounds of all that was going on on the other side of the bushes didn't aid her concentration.

The day of one of the McCords' parties required full staff in addition to outside caterers, waiters and waitresses, bartenders, decorators, florists and extra gardeners. As a child on days like this, Tanya would have been at the heart of it all. She would have had orders to stay out from underfoot, but she would have been put to work running messages from one place to another or doing small odd jobs. It had always been fun and exciting for her.

And then when the party got underway, she would have kept out of sight in the kitchen, watching from there or from behind the bushes when her mother sent her off to bed and she'd hidden there instead of minding her mom.

But today she was nowhere. She wasn't enjoying the bustle and camaraderie of the staff as they did their jobs. She wasn't getting to see everything come together. And she wouldn't spend tonight in the kitchen or sitting in the bushes to watch from the sidelines.

This time around, she was missing out on it all and that added to the sadness she was already wearing like a shroud.

She was sad and melancholy and lonely and miserable and tied up in knots—that's how what had happened with Tate yesterday had left her.

And yet her mother had been so calm about it....

Was that only an act to make me feel better? Tanya wondered as she stared into space rather than at any of her papers.

She knew her mother well and she didn't think that JoBeth had been hiding her true response to spare Tanya. Her mother hadn't seemed at all upset or worried or even unnerved by this turn of events or what could come of it. And if it wasn't a big deal to her mother, should it be such a big deal to her? she asked herself.

Maybe not *such* a big deal—at least when it came to her mother's job. But the fact that JoBeth could come to grips with the idea of Tanya being with Tate still didn't remove the whole problem.

It would still be strange for me, she thought.

As strange as it had been to be at Tate's country club, at the charity dinner, surrounded by the people who had always been a part of his life, by his family. A family *served* by her mother and other people who were like *her* family. How could she be a part of both sides?

Just thinking about it felt awkward, even if JoBeth *had* taken it in stride.

But it was her mother who had suggested that maybe Tanya and Tate could carve out a place of their own and that caused Tanya to recall something that had occurred to her on Thursday night after that steamy kiss they'd shared—that when they were together it *was* in some kind of no-man's-land between their two worlds.

But even if they *could* carve out a place of their own between the two, there would still be times when she would have to venture into the McCord circle....

Okay, so she'd handled Friday night's charity dinner all right, and while she hadn't been received with open arms and warm hugs, there hadn't been any open hostility or snubbing, either. If it was always like that, would it be unbearable? she asked herself.

It wouldn't be, she decided. And really, as a reporter, she was often met with some reservation. So what if the country-club set didn't embrace her and usher her into their ranks? She didn't want to be there anyway and as long as she wasn't shunned, she could live with aloof courtesy. Plus, socializing with the movers and shakers might even give her inside information here and there that she could use—in that way it could even be good for her career.

But country-club events weren't staffed by her mother and a whole lot of other people Tanya was close to. What about *those* times? Times that were purely personal? When her career wouldn't enter into it?

She thought about that. Thought about her mother's comment about introducing JoBeth to the governor.

Yes, if Tanya met the governor she'd be thrilled to turn around and introduce her mother. She certainly wouldn't be embarrassed or feel the least bit ashamed.

So maybe when it came to occupying a new position here, it was all in the attitude. And since Tanya felt certain that she would always have the same attitude toward the people who worked for the McCords, then maybe an alteration in roles was just something minor to be dealt with. Something slightly weird that would become normal, the way her mother had said of her own position....

The more she thought about that, the more doable it seemed.

But what *wasn't* only something to be dealt with was Tate himself.

Were the changes in him permanent? Could she trust that he *had* come to the point where he was finished with Katie Whitcomb-Salgar....

The musicians must have arrived because Tanya heard the tuning of instruments begin.

The party would start soon.

Tate would be there.

Katie Whitcomb-Salgar would be there.

And the mere idea of that tightened the knots in Tanya's stomach and somehow made everything she was mentally sorting through feel all the more in immediate need of a resolution.

Were the changes in Tate permanent? Or would he go back to being the carefree, insulated, good-time-Charlie he'd been before?

She'd told Tate that it seemed to her that the changes in him were really only that he'd grown up, matured. She honestly believed that. And those weren't things that were likely to revert.

Plus, she thought that his eyes genuinely had been opened, and to more than his feelings for her the way he'd said on Sunday morning. And now that they were, now that he felt so strongly about what he'd witnessed and experienced, was it conceivable that he would close his eyes to it all again and be able to forget about it, to go blithely on?

She didn't think that *was* conceivable.

What she'd learned about him was that he had a determination to do more, to help more. Yes, he still needed to reconcile his guilt over having so much himself, but to go back to his carefree ways? That just didn't seem like what the man he was now would do.

No, the more she thought about it, the

more convinced she was that the Tate who had evolved out of the sorrow of losing his friend, the Tate who had gone to the Middle East to contribute what he could, was also the Tate who had returned home determined to continue to contribute here. And *that* was the real Tate now. The Tate he would be from here on.

The Tate who had impressed her and earned her admiration. The Tate who had won her over.

But there was still Katie Whitcomb-Salgar....

The last thing on his mind—that's what her mother had overheard him yell at Blake.

And how many times, in how many ways, had he told Tanya that his relationship with Katie was over?

More times, in more ways, than she could recall.

And if she tried to plug the new Tate into the old pattern of on-again, off-again with Katie?

Tanya had to admit that it didn't line up.

The old Tate was easily swayed. He'd gone whatever way the wind blew. So whenever the wind had blown him back in Katie's direction, he'd merely gone with it.

But the new Tate was firm in his con-

victions. Plus it seemed as if he'd gotten to
know himself on a deeper level. To recognize things not only about life beyond the
walls of the mansion and the country club,
but about himself, too.

And one of the things he'd said he recognized was that he and Katie were nothing more than friends. And never would be
anything more than that....

Tanya wanted to believe that so much it
hurt.

But a breakup of Tate and Katie that actually stuck? That was the hardest for her
to bank on when he'd gone back to Katie so
many other times....

But he swore it's me he wants, not her....

And the truth was, Tanya wanted him too
much not to hang her every hope on believ-
ing that, too.

Because if her mother was right, that where
there's a will there's a way, Tanya definitely
had the will to be with Tate. And if the way
was to accept that he meant what he'd said
when he'd told her he was through with Katie,
then that was what Tanya had to do.

She just had to.

To do anything else was to deny herself Tate.

And more than anything in her entire life, *he* was what she wanted.

And if she could have what she wanted, she should....

That was something else her mother had said and suddenly Tanya was in complete agreement.

She nearly jumped up from the kitchen table and ran for the bungalow's front door.

Then she heard the strains of music coming from the other side of the bushes.

Somewhere in the midst of being lost in her own head, the party had begun....

That's where Tate would be now. And in order to get to him, to see him, to tell him she'd changed her mind, the party was where she would have to be, too.

"So I guess I'm going to my first McCord private party as an invited guest," she said as she took a deep breath to steady herself.

But then she realized how she was dressed.

Her mother had said that the invitations had recommended casual dress, but cutoffs, a tank top and her hair in a ponytail were a little too casual.

Besides, she didn't want to be anywhere near Katie Whitcomb-Salgar without looking her best.

"Just a little while longer," she muttered to herself as she spun on her heels and made a dash for the shower.

Just a little while longer before she could find Tate and tell him that if it wasn't too late—and if he'd really been asking her to marry him—the answer just might be yes....

Chapter Fourteen

Flowered halter sundress. Three-inch high-heel sandals. Slightly less than on-camera makeup. Hair washed, dried and left flowing loosely around her bare shoulders—that was how Tanya left her mother's house and went into the Labor Day evening where darkness had fallen and the white glow of bright party lights lit the night on the other side of the bushes.

Music was playing and the muffled sound of voices and laughter drifted to her as she stepped onto the path that cut through the bushes and trees separating the McCord mansion from her mother's bungalow.

Her shower and party preparations had been tinged with doubts and concerns about everything from the possibility that Tate might have had second thoughts about her by now, to the chance that he *hadn't* been proposing at all and she'd grossly misunderstood him, to the fear that because she'd turned him down he'd already reconnected with Katie.

So as Tanya went along the path she was a bit of a wreck inside.

The closer she got to the McCords' backyard the louder was the music, the voices, the laughter, and the brighter was the glow of light from beyond the path.

That bright glow cast deeper shadows from the bushes and trees and Tanya was startled to suddenly happen upon two people in a small clearing almost at the path's end. Two people standing facing each other, talking intently enough to be unaware of her.

Tanya hesitated. She had to pass by that clearing to get to the party. To Tate. But by then she could tell the people were a man and a woman, and although she couldn't hear what they were discussing, they were very involved in it.

Plus, there was something familiar about

the man's broad-shouldered back that gave her pause....

Then the woman moved inches to one side and Tanya caught enough of a glimpse of her to realize who it was.

Katie Whitcomb-Salgar....

And if that was Katie standing in a relatively private cove with a broad-shouldered man....

Tanya held her breath. She thought her heart actually stopped beating as the worst-case scenario flooded through her mind.

Was Tate the man whose back she was staring at? The man with Katie?

Were they getting together again?

Was that what they were talking about?

Frozen now with her own fears, as Tanya looked on, the man took a step forward, closer to Katie Whitcomb-Salgar.

They could just be talking, Tanya reasoned.

But what if there was more to it....

She didn't want to witness it if there was. If it was Tate with Katie.

Should she make her presence known?

Or should she just turn around and go back to her mother's house? Should she forget everything about this last week with

Tate? Everything he'd said to her? That he may have proposed to her? Should she ignore everything she'd hashed through this afternoon? Everything that had brought her here to talk to him?

Better that, better that he never know she'd changed her mind, better that she salvage her pride if he was proving that she'd been wrong to decide to trust him. To believe that he really had grown or matured. To believe that he had meant it when he'd said he was finished with Katie....

Hot tears flooded Tanya's eyes and she hated herself for being so gullible....

And then there was another adjustment in the positions of the two people she was spying on. The man shifted and turned, putting him in profile, allowing her to see that it wasn't Tate with Katie.

It was Blake....

It was Blake!

Tanya blinked away her tears, realizing at that moment that she was just being a basket case. She had no idea why Blake would be in a somewhat secluded spot with his brother's former fiancée but she didn't care. The only thing she cared about was that it *wasn't* Tate.

She let out the breath she'd been hold-

ing, veered far enough off the path for Katie
and Blake not to see her as she slipped past
them, and then there she was, at the end of
the path, peering into a sea of Dallas's elite
and the people serving them.

But there was only one face she was
searching for in the crowd. That one face
she wanted to wake up to every morning
for the rest of her life....

And then she spotted it.

Tate was standing near the guesthouse's
front door. Alone, looking out over the festivities, removed from them.

He was dressed in slacks and a sport shirt.
He had a drink in his hand, but his expression said he was only going through the mo-
tions. And not putting much effort into even
that.

Tanya summoned strength with another
deep breath and stepped off the path's edge
and into the crowd, making her way through
it with her eyes trained on Tate.

Please don't let it be too late....

She was several yards away when he saw
her coming. His eyes opened wider, his brows
arched. But he didn't smile. He just watched
her close the distance between them and she

knew that repairing things was going to be up to her....

"Hi," she said when she reached him, hating the quavery tone in her voice and hoping he hadn't been able to hear it over the music and the party sounds.

He didn't return her greeting. He merely raised his eyebrows higher, acknowledging her that way but offering no more than that.

"I wondered if we could talk," she said, not knowing what else to do but get right to the point.

"If you're worried about your job or your mother's, don't be. In fact, when it comes to your job, I just talked to Chad Burton—"

"The station owner of WDGN is here?"

Tate nodded in the direction of the crowd of guests. But Tanya didn't want to look away from him. As important as her career was to her, at that moment it wasn't as important as he was, as what she'd come to talk to him about.

Still, before she'd said anything else, Tate said, "I told him to put you back on the air."

"You did?"

"He thinks there's enough material to stretch out your reports, to start them with family history and go from there. I agreed.

I'm just hoping that you won't burn us—that you'll keep any information on the diamond for a big finish only if and when we find it."

He was trusting her. That meant more to her than the fact that she was getting her job back. And it also brought her around again to what she really wanted to say to him.

"Thank you," she said first. "But my job and my mother's job aren't what I came to talk about."

"What did you come to talk to me about?" he asked in a challenging tone.

"I wanted to talk about us...." If there *was* an us... "Could we go somewhere quiet? And private?"

His expression remained blank but he motioned with his glass to the guesthouse.

Tanya's heart was back to beating like a drum as she preceded him to the door. Since it was his home, she waited for him to open it and only went in when he said, "Go ahead."

She stepped into the guesthouse where a single table lamp was the only light and it was actually dimmer inside than it was outside.

Tate came in after her, closing the door behind them, muting the noises. And suddenly Tanya was on the spot without being sure what she was going to say.

She walked as far as the island counter that separated the kitchen and the living area, turning to lean against it and grab on tight to the granite's edge on either side of her hips as if she needed anchoring.

But before she'd thought how to proceed from there, Tate set his glass on an end table half the room away from her and said, "So there's an *us?* You told me at the planetarium that there wasn't."

"I hope now that there is. Or can be," Tanya admitted.

"It was you who didn't want there to be," he reminded her.

"It isn't that I didn't *want* there to be an us," she amended. "I was just...worried about what it might mean if I let there be."

"But now you aren't worried?"

"Well, less," she admitted with a nervous laugh, thinking that she couldn't in all honesty say she was completely unconcerned after the scare she'd just had on the way here.

"But I talked to my mother," she continued, going on to tell him what she and JoBeth had discussed, how JoBeth's support had cleared the way to rethinking everything else that had caused her stance on Sunday morning.

"You said I gave you a new perspective—but I guess I needed one myself," she concluded when she'd told him the whole thing. "But maybe you should tell me how you see things after having a little more time to think about it,"

"There's only one thing I see, Tanya," he said, coming to stand in front of her, taking her upper arms in his hands. "What I see is you and that I want you. A life with you. Close to my family or far away from it—all I want is you. I told you, the details can be sorted out. The only thing that's important to me is that you and I are together."

"In what way, exactly?" she asked quietly, tentatively, because as good as what he'd said sounded, it still wasn't a proposal.

He broke into a slow, one-sided smile. "What do you think?"

"I think you were asking me to marry you yesterday morning, but maybe not and I don't want to accept a proposal that isn't one."

A wide grin spread over his handsome face and obliterated even the last remnant of the dour expression she'd been greeted with.

"It was a proposal yesterday. It's a proposal today. I love you, Tanya. I want you to be my wife."

"I'd like to be your wife," Tanya said, intending it to sound more lighthearted but instead her voice had come out quietly and heartfelt.

And in response Tate's grin became a soft smile just before he pulled her toward him and leaned to meet her so he could kiss her as if it had been far too long since the last time.

Or maybe that was just how it seemed to Tanya as his arms came around her and hers went around him, and she melted into him, starved for that kiss, for him.

Almost instantly the kiss wasn't only a kiss that reunited them and sealed their commitment, though. It was a kiss that sparked a hunger in them both and ignited a flame of passion.

Passion that quickly had his hands on her eager breasts.

But when he untied the halter from around her neck, Tanya reluctantly broke away, holding her top in place with one hand pressed to her chest.

"The party…" she reminded him breathlessly.

"...can go on without us for a while." Tate finished her sentence before he retook her mouth with his.

Tanya couldn't refuse herself what he was offering in favor of any party. Or anything else she could think of as her mind emptied of everything but the wonders of Tate's mouth on hers, of his hands on her bare breasts, of her hands unfastening the buttons of his shirt as fast as she could.

The island counter was the perfect height and once clothes had been flung aside, Tate lifted Tanya onto it, making good use of it. Still kissing, and with her legs wrapped around his hips, and hands exploring and tantalizing, nothing penetrated their absorption in each other or the tiny universe of pleasure that surrounded them and carried them away.

Until the pinnacle had been achieved and the sounds of the party in full swing just outside the guesthouse seeped back into Tanya's consciousness.

"I hope you locked that door," she said with her forehead resting on his shoulder as if it were a shelf.

He nipped at her collarbone and said, "I don't think I did."

"So anybody—one of your family—could just walk in any minute looking for you...."

That made him laugh. "I guess they could."

Tanya pushed away from him and crossed her arms over her bare breasts. "We have to get dressed and go out there before that happens."

Tate placed a sweet, sexy kiss on each of her breasts where they bulged above her arms. "I could lock it now and we could take our time..." he offered, sucking lightly on the side of her neck.

"I think it's better if we can slip out of here before anyone comes looking for you and finds the door locked or unlocked."

He took a deep breath and sighed it out in a warm gust that brushed her bare skin. "The voice of reason—how much fun is that?" he said before he kissed her again and gave her second thoughts about having him lock the door after all.

But then he stopped kissing her and lifted her off the countertop. "I suppose I should track your mother down anyway and ask for your hand in marriage," he pretended to concede against his will.

The idea of him asking her mother for her

hand in marriage made it Tanya's turn to grin. "Have I told you that I love you?" she asked him when the feeling welled up in her so much she couldn't contain it.

Tate kissed her, a brief peck of a kiss, and said, "No, but now that you finally have, I'll want to hear it at least seven times a day, every day."

"Should we make a schedule?" she joked as they both began to gather their clothes and dress again.

"I think spontaneity might be nicer."

Which he proved when he used the time during which he was buttoning his shirt to kiss her neck again and say, "But I *do* love you, Tanya Kimbrough. More than you'll ever know."

After a few swipes of his brush through both of their hair and a little damage control of her makeup, they shared one more long, lingering kiss before they did as Tanya had suggested and slipped back into the Labor Day festivities.

As they did Blake was in the process of quieting the music so he could take over the microphone at center stage.

When he had, he said, "On behalf of my

mother and the rest of my family, we want to welcome everyone here tonight."

Tanya was surprised when Tate moved to stand directly behind her where he wrapped his arms around her, holding her tightly against him and propping his chin on top of her head.

With wide eyes, Tanya glanced around to see if anyone was looking. But no one seemed to be taking any notice and since it was so nice to be there like that with him, so nice to be publicly claimed by him, she just curled her own arms up and clamped her hands around his forearms.

"...I also wanted to take this opportunity," Blake was saying, "to say congratulations to my cousin Gabby and her new husband, Rafe—who have just come back from their honeymoon in Italy." Blake held up his glass in toast as he went on. "Rafe, we're happy to have you as a part of the family now."

Applause and congratulations went up all around and Tanya was heartened somewhat by the warmth that went with it. The man Blake was so openly admitting into the McCord clan was Rafael Balthazar, who had been employed by the McCords to provide security for McCord's Jewelers and, more recently, as Gabby McCord's bodyguard. If the security consultant and bodyguard could become a McCord without anyone wincing, maybe Tate marrying the house-keeper's daughter wouldn't be so difficult to accept either....

But as Blake urged Gabby and Rafe to join him on stage, and the crowd chimed in their encouragement, Tanya looked out over the splendor that was the McCord home and lifestyle and knew in her heart that it didn't make any difference if she was ever truly a part of it.

The only thing she wanted to be a part of was what she and Tate would have together. The rest was nothing more than the border around the edges of the bigger picture.

And as she stood there, fitted to him as if they were meant to come together as one, the last of her doubts, of her fears and worries, seemed to float off in the evening breeze.

Because at that moment she knew deep down that nothing he could have ever had with anyone else, nothing thrust upon him, nothing he'd drifted in and out of, could be anything like what the two of them had found with each other.

And that what the two of them had found with each other really would hold them steady through family approvals and disapprovals, through feuds and diamond hunts and lost treasures and financial woes. Through anything that they had to face.

For a lifetime that they had already begun to carve out together.

* * * * *

WESTERN WP PROMISES

YES! Please send me **The Western Promises Collection** in Larger Print. This collection begins with 3 FREE books and 2 FREE gifts (gifts valued at approx. $14.00 retail) in the first shipment, along with the other first 4 books from the collection! If I do not cancel, I will receive 8 monthly shipments until I have the entire 51-book Western Promises collection. I will receive 2 or 3 FREE books in each shipment and I will pay just $4.99 US/ $5.89 CDN for each of the other four books in each shipment, plus $2.99 for shipping and handling per shipment. *If I decide to keep the entire collection, I'll have paid for only 32 books, because 19 books are FREE! I understand that accepting the 3 free books and gifts places me under no obligation to buy anything. I can always return a shipment and cancel at any time. My free books and gifts are mine to keep no matter what I decide.

272 HCN 3070 472 HCN 3070

Name _____ (PLEASE PRINT) _____

Address _____ Apt. # _____

City _____ State/Prov. _____ Zip/Postal Code _____

Signature (if under 18, a parent or guardian must sign)

Mail to the **Reader Service:**
IN U.S.A.: P.O. Box 1867, Buffalo, NY 14240-1867
IN CANADA: P.O. Box 609, Fort Erie, Ontario L2A 5X3

* Terms and prices subject to change without notice. Prices do not include applicable taxes. Sales tax applicable in N.Y. Canadian residents will be charged applicable taxes. This offer is limited to one order per household. All orders subject to approval. Credit or debit balances in a customer's account(s) may be offset by any other outstanding balance owed by or to the customer. Please allow 4 to 6 weeks for delivery. Offer available while quantities last. Offer not available to Quebec residents.

WPBPA16R

REQUEST YOUR FREE BOOKS!
2 FREE NOVELS PLUS 2 FREE GIFTS!

⊞ HARLEQUIN®

SPECIAL EDITION
Life, Love & Family

YES! Please send me 2 FREE Harlequin® Special Edition novels and my 2 FREE gifts (gifts are worth about $10). After receiving them, if I don't wish to receive any more books, I can return the shipping statement marked "cancel." If I don't cancel, I will receive 6 brand-new novels every month and be billed just $4.74 per book in the U.S. or $5.49 per book in Canada. That's a savings of at least 12% off the cover price! It's quite a bargain! Shipping and handling is just 50¢ per book in the U.S. and 75¢ per book in Canada.* I understand that accepting the 2 free books and gifts places me under no obligation to buy anything. I can always return a shipment and cancel at any time. Even if I never buy another book, the two free books and gifts are mine to keep forever.

235/335 HDN GH3Z

Name	(PLEASE PRINT)
Address	Apt. #
City	State/Prov.	Zip/Postal Code

Signature (if under 18, a parent or guardian must sign)

Mail to the **Reader Service:**
IN U.S.A.: P.O. Box 1867, Buffalo, NY 14240-1867
IN CANADA: P.O. Box 609, Fort Erie, Ontario L2A 5X3

Want to try two free books from another line?
Call 1-800-873-8635 or visit www.ReaderService.com.

* Terms and prices subject to change without notice. Prices do not include applicable taxes. Sales tax applicable in N.Y. Canadian residents will be charged applicable taxes. Offer not valid in Quebec. This offer is limited to one order per household. Not valid for current subscribers to Harlequin Special Edition books. All orders subject to credit approval. Credit or debit balances in a customer's account(s) may be offset by any other outstanding balance owed by or to the customer. Please allow 4 to 6 weeks for delivery. Offer available while quantities last.

Your Privacy—The Reader Service is committed to protecting your privacy. Our Privacy Policy is available online at www.ReaderService.com or upon request from the Reader Service.

We make a portion of our mailing list available to reputable third parties that offer products we believe may interest you. If you prefer that we not exchange your name with third parties, or if you wish to clarify or modify your communication preferences, please visit us at www.ReaderService.com/consumerchoice or write to us at Reader Service Preference Service, P.O. Box 9062, Buffalo, NY 14240-9062. Include your complete name and address.

HSE15

REQUEST YOUR FREE BOOKS!
2 FREE NOVELS PLUS 2 FREE GIFTS!

◆ HARLEQUIN®

American Romance®

LOVE, HOME & HAPPINESS

YES! Please send me 2 FREE Harlequin® American Romance® novels and my 2 FREE gifts (gifts are worth about $10). After receiving them, if I don't wish to receive any more books, I can return the shipping statement marked "cancel." If I don't cancel, I will receive 4 brand-new novels every month and be billed just $4.74 per book in the U.S. or $5.49 per book in Canada. That's a savings of at least 12% off the cover price! It's quite a bargain! Shipping and handling is just 50¢ per book in the U.S. and 75¢ per book in Canada.* I understand that accepting the 2 free books and gifts places me under no obligation to buy anything. I can always return a shipment and cancel at any time. Even if I never buy another book, the two free books and gifts are mine to keep forever.

154/354 HDN GHZZ

Name	(PLEASE PRINT)	
Address		Apt. #
City	State/Prov.	Zip/Postal Code

Signature (if under 18, a parent or guardian must sign)

Mail to the **Reader Service**:
IN U.S.A.: P.O. Box 1867, Buffalo, NY 14240-1867
IN CANADA: P.O. Box 609, Fort Erie, Ontario L2A 5X3

Want to try two free books from another line?
Call 1-800-873-8635 or visit www.ReaderService.com.

* Terms and prices subject to change without notice. Prices do not include applicable taxes. Sales tax applicable in N.Y. Canadian residents will be charged applicable taxes. Offer not valid in Quebec. This offer is limited to one order per household. Not valid for current subscribers to Harlequin American Romance books. All orders subject to credit approval. Credit or debit balances in a customer's account(s) may be offset by any other outstanding balance owed by or to the customer. Please allow 4 to 6 weeks for delivery. Offer available while quantities last.

Your Privacy—The Reader Service is committed to protecting your privacy. Our Privacy Policy is available online at www.ReaderService.com or upon request from the Reader Service.

We make a portion of our mailing list available to reputable third parties that offer products we believe may interest you. If you prefer that we not exchange your name with third parties, or if you wish to clarify or modify your communication preferences, please visit us at www.ReaderService.com/consumerschoice or write to us at Reader Service Preference Service, P.O. Box 9062, Buffalo, NY 14240-9062. Include your complete name and address.

HARI5